SHARING DEL

RAMONA GRAY

EK PUBLISHING INC.

Edited by:
L. Nunn Editing

Cover design by
EK Designs

SHARING DEL

I'm not a good girl. I've spent the last five years screwing all the wrong men and making all the wrong choices. So, when the tall, quiet and gorgeous Cash saves me from a sticky situation, you can bet your ass I did what I always do. Sure, riding Cash like a damn pony feels like the right move in more ways than one, but bad decisions have a way of sneaking up on a girl.

Only, there's more to Cash than meets the eye. Like his relationship with his roommate and best friend Jesse. It's easy to see they're close, and one hot, unforgettable night, I find out exactly how close they are.

Now I have two men in my bed, each very willing to bring me more pleasure than I ever could have imagined. I know it's wrong to want both of them. But, hell, it's just another bad decision in a lifetime of bad choices.

I'm not falling in love with two men. Am I?

CHAPTER 1

I'm twenty-five years old and I'm not a nice girl. Even my mama says I'm not nice. When I was sixteen, she sat me down and told me I was going to Hell. Told me that if I didn't see the light and walk the straight and narrow, God would strike me down with every bit of righteous vengeance he possessed.

At the time, I just chalked it up to her being mad. She had, after all, just caught me sucking Tommy Robertson's cock in the confessional booth at our church. I can't help it. I like boys. I like them a lot. I'm not really into what you would call monogamous relationships. I've tried. I swear to Mother Mary, I've tried, but after a few weeks or a few months, I get bored and I'm moving on to my next conquest.

I tried girls for a while. Figured maybe my problem wasn't committing to one person but committing to one man. I hooked up with a bad girl named Raquel in my first year of college. Oh my sweet blazing Jesus, could that bitch eat pussy. I mean, the girl's tongue was *magic*.

Turns out, though, my issue wasn't with men. After only a few months, I was starting to get bored. I would have left Raquel if she hadn't left me first. Well, maybe her leaving me isn't exactly right. I packed my stuff and left when I came home one night and found her tongue-deep in the pussy of her lab partner. She called me a few times begging for forgiveness, and I told her it was fine. I didn't tell her I was about to leave her anyway.

Even though she cheated on me, I didn't want to hurt her feelings, and I'm kind of worried, you know? Worried that there's something wrong with me that I can't commit to just one person. I have three older sisters, and all of them are happily married to good Catholic boys and popping out babies like they alone are responsible for keeping the Earth's population going.

Last weekend, I visited my oldest sister, Angela. I left the city and headed for the suburbs, saying a silent prayer every few miles that my rust bucket of a car would make it. I sat at the dinner table, two toddlers clinging to my legs and a baby throwing up on my shirt and listened as Angela lectured me.

"Del, you're going to kill Mama and Daddy. You know that, right? They worry about you constantly. Mama spends all her time at Mass praying for your eternal soul. You need to find the right person, settle down and have babies. Children complete your life – trust me on this."

I rolled my eyes and wiped at the spit-up on my shirt. "Yeah, this feels like a really great time."

Angela frowned and took the baby, cooing softly to him before wiping his face clean with the hem of her shirt. "I mean it, Del. Daddy's been having anxiety attacks, and Mama hardly sleeps at night. At least come to church with us once a month."

Good old Catholic guilt. It's alive and well in my family. My parents have seven children, and I'm smack dab in the middle and the only one they fret about. My baby brother Mitchell gave them some trouble for a few months in high school, but they straightened him out pretty quick. I'm the only one they never could figure out or fix. The fate of my eternal soul causes them a lot of heartache.

Of course, my eternal soul was the last thing I needed to be worrying about right now. Paying my rent, eating more than one meal a day – now those were the things that I really needed to concentrate on.

I moved to the city on a whim. I was tired of living in my parents' basement in the suburbs. I was tired of listening to lectures about why I failed at college and in relationships. Hell, why I failed at life.

I worked at a dive bar on 17th Avenue. My tiny apartment on 5th Street had walls so thin you could hear my neighbour Jerry whacking off every night to reruns of the goddamn Golden Girls. My job and shitty apartment weren't in the best areas in the city, but I carried my mace and knew how to use it.

The problem is that I was barely scraping by to begin with, and now my landlord has decided to raise the rent. Nine hundred bucks a month for a shit-ass apartment so tiny I could barely turn around in it without banging into the walls. Nine hundred bucks so I could take a two-minute shower before the water turns cold. Nine hundred bucks to watch mold growing on the walls and listen to an old balding man named Jerry cry out Bea fucking Arthur's name in orgasmic pleasure every goddamn night.

I wasn't going to miss it. Well… maybe Jerry.

I had two weeks left before I needed to move, and I hadn't found anything in my budget. It left me with two choices – take a second job or get a new apartment with a roommate. I chose a second job because, honestly? I didn't play well with others. Except I hadn't found anything yet, and time was rapidly running out.

"Del! You thinking of working tonight or ya just gonna stand there diddlin' yourself?"

I scowled at the bartender. Mark could be a real asshole sometimes. The owner, Bill, wasn't around a lot, and Mark liked to pretend that he ran the place. I adjusted my short skirt, picked up my tray of drinks, and crossed the crowded bar.

It was Saturday night, and things were about to get busy. Once a month, Bill brought in a local band named "Killjoy" to play. They always brought in a huge crowd. Their lead singer, Jesse, had vocals of gold and filled out a pair of leather pants better than any man I knew. The first few months, I seriously considered trying to get into those leather pants, but after watching the groupies throw their panties on stage and flash their tits, I stopped even considering it.

Not that I don't have a kickass body. I might be short, but I'm curvy in all the right spots with a set of tits on me that could make a grown man cry. I've got long dark hair, bright blue eyes and thanks to my mama's side of the family, milky-white skin. Maybe if I weren't about to be homeless, I'd have thought harder about seducing Jesse.

I set down all the mugs of beer but one at a table full of frat boys.

"Sweetheart, you get better looking every time you walk over here." The leader of the group grinned at me with perfect white teeth. He was cute in a frat boy, bratty kind of way. I briefly considered taking him home and showing him the night of his life, but then rejected the idea. Fucking some random guy was no way to avoid my problems. Besides, he was too pretty for me. I liked them big and rough. Still, it didn't mean I couldn't flirt my way into big tips.

"Why, thank you, handsome," I purred and leaned over him, letting him get a good look down my shirt at my tits before I plucked the bills from his hand.

I turned to walk away, and when he smacked me on the ass, I rolled my eyes before turning and giving him a wink. "You'd better watch it, big boy. You never know what I'll do with that hand."

"You can do anything you want to it, sweetheart." The frat boy grinned again as his friends laughed loudly.

I walked away and set the last beer down on the table in the corner farthest from the stage. "Hello, Cash."

"Del." The big man nodded and took a drink of beer before handing me a few bills. I counted out the change and held it out to him, but he shook his head. I nodded gratefully and shoved the bills into my apron pocket.

Cash came in once or twice a month and always sat in my section. He was quiet, kept his hands to himself and was a big tipper. My favourite kind of customer. I waited a moment to see if he would take a look at my tits, but his gaze had already shifted to the stage where the band was starting to set up.

I headed back toward the bar. Cash never looked at my tits, never made rude comments and never drank more than three beers. At first, it kind of bugged me that he never made a pass, but after a while, I found it refreshing. Not that I wouldn't have taken him up on it if he had. I mean, the man practically screamed sex, and he was exactly the kind of man I liked. Big and broad shouldered, with a permanent five o'clock shadow and tanned skin. Dark eyes and full lips, and if he didn't have a nice, hairy chest that a girl could run her fingers through, I'd eat my own apron. He always wore a scuffed leather jacket with a tight t-shirt, jeans and worn cowboy boots. Once when I had snuck out back for a cigarette near the end of my shift, I had seen him leaving on a motorcycle, a big old Harley that roared in the cool night air.

My pussy pulsed at the thought of riding behind Cash, and my panties were suddenly wet. Christ, I really did need to get laid. I didn't have a chance with Cash, but the frat boy was starting to look better and better. There were sudden shrieks, and I knew without looking that Jesse and the rest of Killjoy had taken the stage.

I leaned against the bar and watched for a few minutes. Jesse was wearing his usual leather pants, only this time he had decided to go without the shirt. He usually ended up half-naked before the show was over anyway, so I guess he decided it was pointless even to wear one. As he swayed in time to the music, I studied his upper torso. He was lean and absolutely ripped. Forget six pack, the man had a goddamn eight pack. His nipple rings glinted in the light, and I thought about how nice it would be to pull on those rings with my teeth.

I shook my head. Jesus, I needed to get control of myself. My panties were soaked through, and I was still leaking. I caught the eye of the frat boy, and he gave me a wide grin. I smiled back. Frat boy wasn't my first choice, but he'd do.

———

I SLIPPED OUT THE BACK DOOR OF THE BAR AND STUDIED THE cigarette in my hand. I had quit six months ago, but occasionally bummed one from a co-worker. I lit the cigarette and inhaled deeply. The smoke hit my lungs in a soft rush, and I blew it out gently. God, it had been a long night, and my feet were killing me. I took another puff – I was already feeling a little dizzy from the nicotine – and leaned against the building. I had just finished cashing out and decided to have a quick smoke before I grabbed my things and took off. Frat boy and his friends had disappeared about ten minutes before the bar closed. I was disappointed, but the part of me that wasn't a complete whore knew it was for the best. A night of fucking sounded good, but it wasn't going to solve my problems.

I sighed and took another drag on my cigarette. Tomorrow morning I'd –

"Hello, sweetheart."

I spun around. Frat boy was standing behind me, leaning against the wall and smiling his straight-tooth grin at me.

"Well, hey there." I socked out my hip and lifted the cigarette to my lips. He watched me take a drag, watched the way my lips sucked at the thin white cylinder, and his grin widened.

"Tell me, sweetheart, you got plans after work?"

I shrugged. "Depends."

"Depends on what?"

I stubbed out my cigarette and stepped closer. "Depends on you."

He kissed me, his tongue pushing into my mouth immediately. He had a large tongue, and he was too eager and too determined to show me he was a good kisser. I pulled back and wiped my mouth off discreetly. Perhaps tonight wasn't going to be as fun as I thought.

"I've been wanting to kiss you all night." Frat boy grabbed my breast and squeezed it roughly.

"Slow down, handsome." I tugged his hand away. "Not so fast."

He pushed me up against the wall and cupped my breast again. "Please, you've been practically begging me for it all night."

I rolled my eyes, suddenly remembering why I didn't fuck college boys. "Give me a minute to -"

He kissed my neck, his teeth nipping at the skin, and I pushed him away. "I said, slow down."

"Fine," he pouted and crossed his arms over his chest.

"Let me just grab my things and we'll go," I said.

He grinned and glanced behind his shoulder. I followed

7

his gaze, frowning when I saw his three buddies climbing out of the car.

"Do we get a group rate, sweetheart?"

Anger flooded through me, and I spat on him. "I don't do groups, you little prick."

He wiped the spittle off his cheek and looked at the liquid on his fingers in disbelief. "You bitch! Did you spit on me?"

I reached for my can of mace, remembering too late that it was in my jacket in the bar. I backed up in the general direction of the door, glancing around as frat boy and his dickhead buddies drew closer.

"Listen, sweetheart, you'll come back to our place and you'll show us all a good time, okay? In the morning we'll, I don't know, take you out for breakfast or something to say thanks."

"Fuck you, asshole!" I snarled. Without taking my eyes off of them, I reached behind me for the door handle. I cursed under my breath when I felt nothing but the rough brick wall of the bar. Where was the goddamn door?

With surprising speed, frat boy lunged for me. I opened my mouth to scream, and he clamped a hard hand over my mouth. "Don't do that, sweetheart. We just want to -"

He was ripped violently away from me, and I pressed my body against the wall as he was thrown to the ground. He hit the pavement with a loud thud and cursed loudly.

"I don't believe the lady is interested, little boy." Cash towered over him with his hands folded neatly behind his back.

I stared at him in relief. I think this might have been the first time I had seen Cash standing up close, and I was shocked by just how large he was. My small frame was dwarfed by his, and his hands were twice the size of mine.

The frat boy stumbled to his feet with his hands clenched

into fists and backed up until he was standing with his buddies.

"Get out of here, man. This doesn't concern you." He tried to sound tough, but even I could see the way he was trembling.

"Oh, I think it does," Cash replied mildly. "You and your little friends get in your car and get the fuck out of here."

Frat boy glanced at his friends. They nodded, and he grinned at Cash. "There are four of us and only one of you. You're outnumbered, asshole."

Cash didn't reply. I was standing frozen against the wall, my heart beating too fast in my chest, and my mouth tasting like frat boy and cigarettes.

"You know what they say, don't you?" Frat boy sneered. "The bigger they are, the harder they fall."

"Why don't you stop running your mouth and bring it then, little boy?" Cash said quietly.

The frat boys ran forward, and I watched flabbergasted as Cash kicked the shit out of them.

"You okay?" Cash's deep voice washed over me, and I looked away from where the frat boys were lying in a crumpled heap on the cold pavement.

"I – uh, thank you?" I whispered, staring up at him. He wasn't even breathing hard as he zipped up his leather jacket against the cold.

"No problem." He held his hand out to me. "Let's get out of here."

I hesitated. "My stuff is in the bar. My coat and my apartment keys."

"You won't need them tonight. Let's go, Del."

I was reaching for his hand before my name had even left

his mouth. He led me past the moaning frat boys and toward his motorcycle. He swung his leg over it. The line of his thigh in his tight jeans made my mouth water as he beckoned to me.

"Climb on."

I nodded, but before I could climb on behind him, he held out his hand. "Wait." He took his jacket off and bundled me into it. I was grateful for its warmth. My t-shirt was thin, and the air was cold.

"You're going to freeze to death," I said.

He shrugged. "I'll be fine."

He patted the seat behind him, and I hiked up my short skirt until it was just below my ass and swung into the seat. I pushed forward, my crotch jammed firmly against him, and my hands linked tightly around his waist. He started the motorcycle, and I jumped at the roar.

"Ready?" He shouted over the engine.

"Yes!" I shouted back. He lifted the kickstand, the motorcycle swayed, and I squeezed my arms around him as he tore off down the street.

CHAPTER 2

"Where are we?" I climbed off the motorcycle and stared up at the large apartment building.

A young man wearing a red jacket and black dress pants ran out from the lobby of the building.

"Good evening, sir."

"Hello, Bobby. How's the shift tonight?"

Bobby shrugged. "Good. Quiet." He didn't look at me, just held his hand out for the key to the bike.

Cash handed him the key and ushered me toward the front door as behind us, his motorcycle roared to life.

"Where are we?" I repeated and gave Cash a suspicious look.

"We're at my place."

"You live here?" I blinked in surprise at him.

He nodded. "Yes."

"You're shitting me." I craned my neck upward. The building was at least twenty stories high and in the heart of downtown.

"I'm not." He cupped my elbow and led me into the lobby.

"Good evening, Mr. Cash." The doorman nodded politely to me as he opened the door.

"Hello, Warren. How are you?"

"Just fine, thank you, sir."

As Cash led me toward the elevator, I stared up at him. I managed to keep my mouth shut until the elevator doors closed behind us and then blurted out, "Are you rich?"

"I do okay for myself," he said as he inserted a small silver key and pushed the button for the penthouse floor.

"Okay for yourself?" I repeated. The elevator moved smoothly upward, and within less than a minute, we were at the top, and the doors were opening. I leaned back against the wall of the elevator and stared in disbelief, my mouth dropping open. The foyer of his home was larger than my entire apartment.

Cash laughed at the look on my face and took my arm. "Come, little lamb, I'll show you around."

He took his jacket from me and hung it neatly on the coat tree before removing his boots with a grunt. I slipped out of my high heels, sighing softly with relief as my bare feet rested on the cool tile.

"Are you hungry?" Cash took my hand and led me out of the foyer and into the kitchen. He took two bottles of water from the fridge, opened one, and then handed it to me. I shook my head no, staring around at the gleaming counter-tops and stainless steel appliances before taking a drink of water as he guzzled half the water in his bottle.

We left the water bottles on the counter, and he took my hand again and led me through the apartment. "This is the living room."

I peeked inside, my eyes widening at the large fireplace, leather furniture and baby grand piano.

He tugged on my hand and led me down the hallway. "My office and library."

"Holy shit," I muttered. The room was dominated by floor-to-ceiling bookcases, which were stuffed with books. I dropped his hand and entered the room, staring delightedly at the books. I ran my fingers across the spines and inhaled the smell of old books as Cash leaned against the mahogany desk.

"Do you like to read?"

"Yes." I nodded enthusiastically. It was true. I had always been a bookworm.

"I didn't expect that," he said.

I grinned at him and looked down at my tight t-shirt and indecently short skirt. "I don't look much like the reading type, do I?"

He laughed and shook his head. I pulled a book from one of the shelves and leafed through it. It was old and battered, with thin pages.

"This looks like an old book," I said.

"It's over two hundred years old. It's worth four thousand dollars," he said.

I nearly dropped the book. "Jesus. I'm sorry."

"For what?"

"I shouldn't have touched it." I still clutched the book, afraid to even place it back on the shelf.

He shrugged and crossed the room to take the book from me. "Books are supposed to be touched and enjoyed."

He shelved it with a carelessness that made me shudder and then took my hand again. "Come, little lamb."

We walked down the wide hallway, and he pointed to a closed door. "That's the guest bathroom."

He opened the next door, and I peeked inside. "The guest bedroom." He walked past another closed door without comment and led me to the end of the hallway. He opened the double doors and stepped aside so I could enter.

My breath caught in my throat. It was obviously the

primary bedroom. There was a small sitting area in front of the fireplace embedded in the left wall. Two overstuffed chairs flanked the fireplace. French doors led out to what I assumed was a large balcony. The right wall had two doors. One was open, and I could make out the counter and double sinks of the bathroom. But it was the wall opposite us that had caught my attention. It was made entirely of glass, and the largest bed I had ever seen was situated in front of it. It seemed weird to have a bed in the middle of the room, but I could see why he did it. The view out the giant glass wall from his bed would be breathtaking.

"This is my bedroom."

"It's gorgeous," I spoke in a hushed whisper. The rich opulence of the room had my typically loud and brash personality shrinking into the dust.

"I'm glad you like it." He led me to the glass wall, and I stared at the view of the city. The lights twinkled, and I gave him a look of delight.

"It's so beautiful."

He smiled. "Yes, beautiful."

I swallowed as he stepped closer and brushed his fingers across my cheek. "Very beautiful."

He bent his head and kissed me. I moaned into his mouth as he deepened the kiss. His large hands circled my waist, and he pulled me against him.

"Do you know how long I've wanted you, little lamb?" he whispered into my ear.

I shook my head dazedly. "You never check me out."

He laughed. "I do. I'm just subtler about it than most of the bar patrons."

He cupped my large breast, his thumb circling my nipple. "I want to fuck you, Del. Do you want to fuck me?"

I reached for his t-shirt, tugging at it impatiently in

answer. He pulled it off, and I sucked in my breath at the sight of his large, tanned chest. Like I suspected, it was covered in dark hair, and I ran my fingers through it before tracing his six pack.

"Thank God, I won't have to eat my own apron," I said.

"What?"

"Nothing." I rubbed his chest again.

My gentle touch seemed to break his control, and he was ripping my t-shirt over my head and unhooking my bra with rough impatience. As soon as my large breasts were bared, he bent over and cupped them, lifting them to his mouth and sucking one hard pink nipple into his mouth. He bit it lightly, and I gasped and arched my back.

He pushed me up against the smooth glass, his hands reaching for my skirt. He shoved it up around my waist and tore my panties off with one smooth yank. He dropped the ripped material to the floor and then fell to his knees, burying his face in my crotch and inhaling deeply. I clutched his short dark hair in my hands as he parted my legs and stared at my pussy.

"Such a pretty little pussy." He smiled up at me as his thumbs parted my soaking wet pussy lips and exposed my throbbing clit. He flattened his tongue and licked my pink button. I cried out and hooked my leg around his shoulders as he probed my wet hole with his tongue.

"Cash!" I cried out again, my legs trembling as his hands dug into my thighs and his tongue slid in and out. He licked back up to my clit and sucked it into his mouth as he shoved one thick finger deep inside of my throbbing pussy.

He sucked hard on my clit, his finger pushing in and out of me, and I climaxed explosively around him. I shrieked with pleasure, and as my legs started to buckle, he stood quickly and lifted me against the glass. He held me there with his lower body as he reached into his jeans pocket and pulled out a condom.

He held the package to my mouth. "Open this, little lamb."

I tore into it with my teeth, spitting out the packaging as he pulled the rubber from the package and reached between us. He unzipped his pants and pushed them down around his ankles. He wasn't wearing underwear, and I watched as he rolled the condom onto his cock.

"Jesus Christ, Cash," I said.

His cock was huge, at least ten inches long and thicker than any cock I'd seen before. I thought about that huge cock pushing its way into my willing body, and my pussy actually started dripping.

"Don't be afraid, Del." He gripped the bottom of my thighs with his large hands and lifted me.

"I'm not," I panted. "Fuck me, Cash. Fuck me right now."

He pressed his cock to my opening and pushed. I groaned with pleasure and pain as his stiff shaft entered me.

"Christ, Del, your pussy is so tight," he groaned and shoved a little more of his length in.

I panted and moaned as, inch by torturous inch, he forced my dripping pussy to take his entire cock. When he was finally completely inside of me, he stopped and bent his dark head to take my nipple into his mouth again. He sucked hard on the tip, scraping his teeth across it as I wiggled and stretched around his hard cock. He moved within me, and I cried out again as his cock rubbed against my soft walls. I tried to tighten my muscles around him, but his dick was so thick I could barely squeeze him despite the Kegel exercises I did when I was bored at work. Cash lifted his head and kissed me, licking at the inside of my mouth until I was panting and squeezing his broad shoulders.

"Try again, little lamb. I know it's thick, but try to milk my cock with your pretty little pussy."

I groaned and squeezed again as hard as I could, biting at my bottom lip and feeling a secret thrill when he moaned and twitched inside of me.

"Good girl," he whispered against my mouth. "Now, hang on tight."

He rammed his cock into me, and my back hit the glass wall. The part of me that was worried he would break the glass disappeared under a wave of unbelievable pleasure as he fucked me senseless.

I lost track of how many times I climaxed as he fucked me. When he finally came, arching his back and shouting as he pumped into me, I was as weak as a kitten from the orgasms. He set me down carefully, and I actually wobbled and nearly fell over. He chuckled and kicked off his jeans before carrying me to the bed and stripping me of my skirt. He tucked me into the bed, and I snuggled into his hard, warm chest as he stroked my long, dark hair.

"Sleep, little lamb," he said.

"WAKE UP, DEL." CASH'S DEEP VOICE AND WARM MOUTH coaxed me out of sleep.

I stretched and blinked owlishly at Cash leaning over me.

"What time is it?"

Cash shrugged, his large hand covering my breast and kneading it firmly. "I don't know. Six, maybe?"

"Why are you up so goddamn early?" I grumbled. I wanted to bury myself under the covers and go back to sleep, but his other hand was slipping between my legs and rubbing my pussy.

"I want to fuck you again, little lamb," he whispered into my ear. He stuck his tongue into my ear, and I nearly arched off the bed as he pushed his finger deep into my pussy at the same time.

"Cash, I'm not really a morning person," I moaned.

"You might not be, but your pretty cunt is." He laughed and brought his fingers up to show me. "Look how wet you are already." His fingers glistened with my juices, and he slipped his finger between my lips.

I sucked eagerly, tasting myself on his finger as his cock dug into my hip. He put his hand back between my thighs and rubbed hard, spreading my juices around. When his hand slipped between my ass cheeks and his finger probed at my anus, I clenched my ass shut.

"Have you been fucked in the ass before, Del?" He stared down at me.

"Yes. But not with a dick the size of yours," I said.

"Did you like it?"

I shrugged. "I didn't hate it, but it didn't do much for me. I dated a girl once named Raquel, and if you stuck a vibrator up her ass, she came so hard she would black out."

He didn't seem fazed by my revelation of dating a woman, and I scored him a mental point for it.

"I'd like to fuck you in the ass, Del," he said.

"You're really big, Cash," I pointed out.

"I am," he agreed, "but I'll stop if you don't like it."

I studied him. The last guy I let fuck me in the ass had a pecker half the size of Cash's, and it had still hurt.

"It'll hurt," I said.

"Maybe, but I'll be careful and go slow. I promise."

"Do you have lube?"

He reached behind him into the bedside table. He showed me the bottle of strawberry-flavoured lube, and I grinned at him. "Let the ass-fucking commence."

He leaned down and kissed me, his hard hands touching and caressing every part of my body until I was moaning and bucking under him. He sat up and moved to the edge of the bed. "Come sit on my lap, Del."

Feeling nervous, I crawled to the edge of the bed. He smoothed on a condom, and I straddled his lap. He reached between us and rubbed my clit until I came wildly, my body shuddering and my mouth gasping his name. He turned me around on his lap until my back was to his chest. I tensed when I felt the liquid dripping down the crack of my ass.

"Relax, little lamb. Remember, I'll stop if you don't like it."

He poured even more lube down my ass, rubbing it between my cheeks and over my anus. His finger probed and pushed and then slid easily into my ass. I cried out a little. It didn't hurt. In fact, a thin thread of pleasure slipped through my body. I relaxed against him as he pressed a second finger into my ass. He spent nearly five minutes, probing and stretching my ass as I moaned softly.

I was surprised when he removed his fingers, lifted me and pushed his cock into my pussy. I moaned and squeezed his thighs with my hands as he gripped my waist and moved me easily up and down his large cock.

"God, Del, so tight," he groaned and thrust deeply into me.

I bounced helplessly on his lap as pleasure coursed through my body. I barely noticed when he pulled his cock out of my pussy and guided it to my ass. But when he pushed it against my anus, I twitched and tried to pull away.

"Wait, little lamb." He reached around and cupped my breasts before licking a slow path up my spine. I moaned as his fingers played with my nipples, and when he reached down and rubbed my clit, I relaxed against him. The head of his cock pushed into my ass, and I cried out. There was pain, but not nearly as bad as I feared. Still, he stopped immediately and poured more lube down my ass and onto his cock.

He pulled me back against his broad chest and held me

firmly before he rubbed my clit once more. I panted and moaned and cried out. When I came for a second time, he pushed his cock fully into my ass. The pain blotted out the pleasure, and I dug my nails deep into his thighs. He stayed perfectly still and rubbed my thighs.

"Okay, little lamb?" he murmured into my ear.

"Yes," I whispered. My ass felt stretched and uncomfortable, but the pain had faded. I moved experimentally on top of him.

His breath hissed out between his teeth, and a tingle went through me. "Does that feel good, Cash?"

"Fuck yes," he muttered.

I braced my hands on his thighs and moved my body up and down a little. His hands tightened around my waist, and he helped me move, thrusting his hips back and forth. After only a few minutes, he was plunging in and out of my ass and moaning loudly. I wasn't expecting to feel any pleasure, so when the first beats of it began in my lower body, I gasped and stopped moving.

"What's wrong?" he groaned against my back.

"Nothing. It… it feels good." I blushed. I had no idea why it felt good, but maybe it was the size difference.

"Good." He circled one arm around my waist and held me steady as he thrust in and out. His other hand reached between my legs and played with my clit. The pleasure built inside of me until my entire body was throbbing with it. Cash was breathing heavily behind me, his large cock filling my ass. Without warning, he pinched my clit hard. I came screaming around him, not even realizing he was coming as well until he pulled out of my ass and collapsed on the bed, pulling me down with him.

"I knew you'd like it, little lamb," he said when we finally caught our breath.

I didn't answer as he reached for a remote control on the

bedside table and pushed a button. There was a soft whirring noise, and blinds descended the wall of glass, blocking out the sun that was peeking over the horizon. We were plunged into darkness, and he tucked me under the covers, curling up beside me and cupping my breast in his hand.

CHAPTER 3

I woke up alone in bed a few hours later. I sat up and stretched before making my way to the bathroom. I squealed with delight at the giant tub and large walk-in shower. I used my finger and Cash's toothpaste to brush my teeth the best I could before stepping into the shower. It had multiple shower heads, and I turned the hot water on high and stayed in the shower for a good half-hour. It was a far cry from my two-minute showers at the apartment.

I strode naked through his bedroom and peeked into the closed door next to the bathroom. Like I suspected, it was a walk-in closet, and I quickly grabbed one of Cash's t-shirts and slipped it over my head. It fell past my knees, and I laughed a little. God, he was a big man. My skirt and t-shirt were still crumpled on the floor, and I picked them up and folded them neatly, laying my bra on top of them. My panties were ruined, and I chucked them into the garbage can in the bathroom before easing open the bedroom door.

I could smell bacon and toast, and my stomach grumbled loudly. I hadn't eaten at all yesterday, and the exercise I did with Cash last night meant I was starving. I followed my nose to the kitchen.

Cash was bent over and leaning into the fridge. His ass was sticking out, and I smiled a little before creeping up and grabbing it.

"Good morning, sexy."

Cash's head popped up, and I screamed breathlessly. It wasn't Cash's dark head but Jesse's blond one.

I staggered back, hitting the doorframe as Jesse grinned at me. "Good morning yourself, sexy." He scanned my body slowly, and I was uncomfortably aware of my nakedness under Cash's soft shirt.

"What the fuck are you doing here?" I snapped.

He arched one pierced eyebrow at me. "I live here."

"The fuck you do!" I said.

He set the bag of shredded cheese he was holding on the counter. "The fuck I don't. Cash and I are roommates."

I staggered over to a kitchen chair and sank into it. "He never mentioned it to me."

Jesse shrugged. "Cash doesn't say a lot."

"How long have you been roommates?" I watched as Jesse cracked two eggs into a steel bowl.

"A few years now. What do you want in your omelet?"

"Um…" I looked around. "Where's Cash?"

"He had to go to work. He'll probably be gone all day. Apparently, there's a big merger happening this week."

I frowned. "What does Cash do?" Before I saw his apartment, I assumed he worked construction or some other type of labour job.

"He's the CFO of a big investment company. What do you want in your omelet?" Jesse raised his eyebrow again at me.

"I should probably get going," I said. It felt weird to be sitting in the kitchen watching the lead singer of Killjoy cook me an omelet.

"Don't be silly," Jesse said. "Cash asked me to make you breakfast. He said you'd be hungry."

He winked at me, and I blushed furiously. There was no way Jesse hadn't heard me screaming my pleasure as Cash fucked me in the ass earlier this morning.

"Surprise me," I said. I shifted in the chair and studied Jesse discreetly. He was wearing jeans and a wrinkled t-shirt. His short blonde hair was sticking straight up, and his feet were bare.

"It was a great show last night." I couldn't stand the quiet.

"Thanks." He poured the eggs into the hot pan and turned the bacon. It sizzled loudly as he buttered the toast.

"Do you like to cook?"

"I do," he said. "I cook all of our meals."

He put the toast on the table and poured me a glass of orange juice. He flipped the omelet as he hummed softly to himself. He took a plate, piled the bacon onto it, and then set it in front of me. He slid the omelet onto another plate and set it down with a flourish.

"Your breakfast, m'lady."

I laughed. "Thank you."

He poured himself a cup of coffee and then raised his eyebrow at me.

"Yes, please."

He gave me a mug of the steaming hot liquid. "Do you want cream or sugar?"

I shook my head and took a sip of the rich dark brew. "It's really good."

Jesse nodded. "Yeah, Cash is kind of picky about his coffee." He sat down across from me. "Eat."

"Are you not eating?"

"I already did." He sipped at his coffee as I picked up my fork and took a bite of the omelet.

"This is delicious." I wasn't blowing smoke up his ass. It was probably the best-tasting omelet I'd ever eaten.

"Thanks."

I hesitated and then scarfed down the omelet, toast and bacon. I was starving, and with about twenty bucks to my name, I had no idea when I'd be eating this well again.

Jesse watched me eat with some amusement. "Worked up an appetite, huh?"

"Uh, yeah." I blushed and drank the orange juice in three large gulps.

"Do you like working at the bar?"

I shrugged. "It pays the bills, right?"

"I guess."

I glanced around the large kitchen. "Can I ask you a question, Jesse?"

"Sure." He took a sip of his coffee.

"Why are you playing at a place like Bill's? If Killjoy is doing well enough that you can afford to live in a penthouse downtown, why are you playing at a crappy bar like Bill's?"

Jesse laughed. "In exchange for cooking, Cash cuts me a break on the rent. I still pay rent, just not as much as you'd think."

"How did you meet Cash?"

"At the bar. He's been going there for years."

"And you just decided to move in together?" I took another sip of coffee.

"Why not? Cash is a good guy, and the penthouse is big enough for two. Hell, it's big enough for five." He laughed.

I smiled and finished my coffee. "I should probably get going." I picked up my plate and carried it to the sink. Jesse stood up and moved beside me.

"Here, I'll take that." He reached for the plate. His arm brushed across my breast, and my nipple hardened immediately.

I flushed and stepped back, folding my arms over my tits. "I'm just going to um, get dressed now."

"Sure." Jesse gave me a slow smile, and I swallowed nervously.

"Thanks for breakfast."

"Any time, Del."

"YOU REALLY DON'T HAVE TO DO THIS, JESSE," I SAID AS HE drove out of the underground parking garage.

"I don't mind. Besides, Cash would kill me if I made you take a cab back to your place."

I relaxed against the leather seat. "I like your car."

"It's Cash's," Jesse said cheerfully. "I just borrow it when I need it. Now, where do you live?"

"Actually, if you could just take me to the bar, that would be great. I need to get my keys and my coat."

"How will you get into the bar?"

"Bill will be there. He's always there on Sunday, counting his money from the week."

We drove in silence the rest of the way, and when Jesse pulled up in front of the bar, I gave him a brief smile. "Thanks again, Jesse."

"I'll wait for you."

"Oh, you don't have to. I can take the bus." I rarely drove my car to the bar. I didn't trust that it wouldn't be broken into, and bus fare was cheaper than gas money.

"Nope." Jesse shut off the car. "I'll wait."

I slid out of the car. I really didn't want him to see where I lived. It was too embarrassing. What if he told Cash?

I ran to the bar, spoke briefly with Bill, and then grabbed my things and headed back outside. I hoped Jesse had grown tired of waiting and left. My heart sank. He was still sitting

27

patiently in the parking lot, drumming the steering wheel and singing to himself.

I climbed into the car and fastened my seatbelt as he started the car. "Where to?"

I gave him the directions and stared silently out the window as he turned up the music and sang along. He really did have a great voice, and I glanced at him. He caught my eye and winked. "Sorry, I always sing when I'm in the car."

"I don't mind. Your voice is amazing," I said.

"Thanks." He turned down my street, his brow furrowing a little as he pulled up in front of my building.

"This is where you live?" He peered out the windshield at the homeless man sleeping on the bench outside my building and our local drug dealer standing on the corner.

"Yeah. Thanks for the ride, Jesse. Tell Cash I said thanks, and I'll see him around."

"Does he have your number?"

I smiled a little. "I think last night was a one-time thing for him."

"Are you sure?"

"Yeah, I'm sure. Thanks again for breakfast. I'll see you at the bar next month, okay?"

I scooted out of the car and tugged nervously on my skirt as I climbed the steps to my building. I waved at Jesse and slipped into the foyer of the building. The pungent smell of urine hit my nostrils, and I covered my face with my hand and ran up the stairs to my apartment.

"WHAT ARE YOU GOING TO DO, DEL?" DANA FROWNED AT ME as I took off my apron and tucked it into the locker.

I shrugged. "I don't know. There's a homeless shelter in my neighbourhood. Maybe I'll check that out."

"That's not funny." Dana hung her own apron up in her locker in the staff room.

"Don't worry, Dana. I'll think of something. I always do." I sighed and counted my tip money. For a Saturday night, it was dead, and I had made only sixty bucks in tips. I was exhausted, my feet ached, and I had spent the last two weeks searching for a second job and a more affordable place to live. Nothing had panned out. Tomorrow, I was being kicked out of my apartment, and I had nowhere to go.

That wasn't entirely true. I could always go back to my parents' basement. I shuddered at the thought. I would rather live in my car.

I left the bar, waving goodnight to Dana and trudged wearily to the bus stop. I drew my thin coat closer around my body. It was cold tonight, and clouds were gathering. I sighed and stared at the pavement between my feet. Two weeks ago, I was on the back of Cash's motorcycle and about to have the best sex of my life.

As I suspected, I hadn't heard from or seen Cash since that night. Killjoy would be playing in a couple of weeks, and I wondered if he would show up for that. He rarely missed one of their performances.

As big fat raindrops fell on my head, I sighed. It didn't matter. I had no idea if I'd even be working at Bill's in two weeks. It was hard to keep a job when you were living out of your goddamn car.

CHAPTER 4

"You goddamn prick! Motherfucker! Let me in! My lease isn't up until tomorrow!" I buzzed my landlord's apartment number repeatedly. I held my hand down on the buzzer as I tried again to open the door with my useless key. The bastard landlord had changed the lock while I was at work. He still wasn't answering, and I picked up a rock and threw it at his apartment window. It missed by a mile, and I screamed again with frustration as the cold rain soaked into my shivering body.

I ran behind the building to my car in the parking lot. I muttered a curse when I tried to start it, and nothing happened. The fucking piece of shit had broken down on me again at the worst possible time. It was the fucking sprinkles on my goddamn cake of misery.

I sat in my dead car for a few minutes. I thought about sleeping in it until morning, but the night was getting colder, and I didn't relish the idea of freezing to death. I had a sudden idea and ran back to the building and buzzed Jerry's apartment. After a moment, his raspy voice came booming out of the speaker. "Who's there?"

"Jerry, it's Del. Can you let me in? I'm locked out." I tried to sound nonchalant.

"Sorry, Del, I can't. Todd told me specifically not to let you in. He said your lease is up."

"He's lying, Jerry!" I said. "I have until tomorrow to pack and leave. He's holding my stuff hostage!"

"Todd said you would say that," Jerry said.

I could have smashed my fist into the wall with anger. Instead, I smiled at the speaker. "Jerry, please let me in. It's raining and it's late and you know this is a bad neighbourhood."

"I can't, Del. Todd will kick me out if I do."

"Goddammit!" I shrieked.

A window in the building beside me cracked open, and a man stuck his head out. "Jesus Christ! Shut the fuck up! Some of us are trying to sleep!"

I flipped him the bird as Jerry's voice crackled over the speaker. "I gotta go, Del. Golden Girls is on."

"Jerry, no! Wait! Just let me in, please, I -"

There was a click as Jerry hung up. I kicked the door of the apartment building, wincing and grabbing my foot as pain radiated from my toe into my foot.

"Goddamn it!" I hopped down the steps and began limping in the direction of the homeless shelter. The rain was pouring down so hard I could barely see, and I was completely drenched and freezing my ass off.

"Keep it together, Del," I muttered as I limped down the street. Tomorrow I would swallow my pride and call my mother for bus money back home. Lights flashed behind me, and a car pulled up and parked next to me. I ignored it and kept limping. The last thing I needed was some pervert trying to drag me into his car.

"Del!"

My back stiffened at the familiar voice, and I turned

around slowly. Cash stood next to his car. "Get in."

"What are you doing here?"

"Looking for you."

"How do you know where I live?"

"Jesse told me." He glared at me impatiently. "Get in the goddamn car, Del. I'm getting soaked out here."

I hobbled to the car and climbed in as he ducked into his own seat. We shut the doors, and he stared for a long moment at my wet, shivering body.

"Why are you walking in the rain?" He angled the heat vents at me.

"I find it refreshing." I held my shaking hands out before trying to dry my dripping hair with my equally wet t-shirt.

He stared at me in exasperation, and I shrugged. "Why are you wearing a suit? It's two in the morning."

"I just finished work."

"Just finished work? Don't you work in an office?"

"Yes. It's been hectic the last couple of weeks."

"Oh. Why are you here?" I said. "Are you some weirdo stalker?"

He laughed. "No. I had planned to go to the bar tonight to see you, but I ended up working too late. I texted Jesse for your address and took the chance that you might still be awake and want to have coffee."

"Coffee at two in the morning," I said. "We're both adults, Cash. You can admit that you were looking for a booty call."

He laughed again. "It's ridiculous how much I've missed you the last two weeks, Del."

I studied him silently. I wasn't willing to admit that I had missed him, too. Cash was handsome and amazing in bed, but I wasn't stupid enough to think he wanted anything more than sex.

"Why were you walking in the rain, little lamb?" he asked.

My calm broke at the softly uttered nickname, and I burst

into tears. "My goddamn landlord locked me out of my apartment building. I had until tomorrow before my lease was up, but the asshole changed the locks while I was at work tonight. Plus, my car is dead, and I think I broke my toe when I kicked the door."

I wiped my nose with the back of my hand and looked out the window.

"Do you have anywhere else to go?"

"Yeah." I sniffed. "Could you give me a lift?"

"Yes. Where to?" He pulled into the street.

"Take your first left." We drove mostly in silence, with me muttering the occasional direction until we pulled up in front of the homeless shelter.

He frowned and peered at the building. "What the fuck is this?"

"It's a place for losers like me." I laughed bitterly and unbuckled my seatbelt. "Thanks for the ride, Cash."

His hard hand gripped my arm. "Is this a homeless shelter?"

I didn't reply, and he cursed and pulled back into the street.

"Hey!" I looked behind me at the shelter. "Cash, take me back. Please. I don't have anywhere else to go, okay?"

"Put on your seatbelt, Del," he growled.

"Cash -"

"Put it on." His tone suggested I would be wise not to disobey, and I clicked it into place as he drove down the street.

"Where are we going?" I asked meekly after a few minutes of silence.

"Back to my place."

"Cash, I appreciate that, but I can't stay at your place. I -"

"You're staying with me tonight, Del. Stop arguing with me."

"Good evening, Mr. Cash."

"Hello, Warren."

"Terrible weather tonight, isn't it?"

"It's ugly out," Cash agreed as he ushered me into the building. I was soaking wet and freezing, and I suspected that I looked like a drowned rat. The mirrored wall next to the elevator doors confirmed my suspicions.

Cash and I rode up the elevator in silence. I sniffed miserably and tried to stop the hot tears from leaking down my face. I was mortified that Cash was seeing me like this and even more humiliated that he knew I was homeless.

It was stupid. What did I care what Cash thought of me? We spent one night together. We weren't fucking engaged. Still, the tears continued to leak down my face, and I wiped them away as the elevator doors opened into his foyer. I took off my shoes and dropped my purse on the floor as Cash shrugged out of his jacket and shoes.

"W-where's Jesse?" I stammered through chattering teeth.

Cash shrugged. "At a gig, I think."

He took my hand and led me straight to the primary bathroom. I watched as he turned the shower on, testing the water with his hand before turning back to me. He pulled my wet t-shirt off and undid my bra before tugging my skirt down over my hips. He removed my thong, leaving me naked and shivering and then quickly removed his own clothes.

He led me into the shower, and I stood under the hot spray of the multiple shower heads. He poured shampoo into his hand, washed and rinsed my hair, and then lathered soap in his hands. As his strong hands soaped my soft flesh, the familiar beat of lust started up in my belly.

I sighed with pleasure when he turned me around and soaped my back. I leaned against him, rubbing my wet ass against his erection as he reached around and cupped my breasts. He massaged them gently, rubbing his thumbs over my nipples before pinching them lightly.

"Cash," I moaned as his hand drifted down my belly and traced the soft curls between my thighs.

"I've missed your pretty cunt, little lamb," he whispered into my ear. I parted my legs eagerly, and he stroked my clit gently before sliding two fingers deep into my aching pussy. I humped his hand as he bit and sucked on my throat.

He flicked lightly at my clit with his thumb, and I arched my hips into his hand and climaxed. I fell back against him, panting and feeling almost dizzy with desire. I couldn't believe how quickly he had made me come. It had to be a goddamn record for me.

He turned me around and kissed me deeply, his tongue stroking mine as he put his arms around me and gripped my ass tightly. "It would seem your pretty little cunt missed me too." There was a note of satisfaction in his voice, and he laughed when I blushed.

I didn't know what the hell was happening to me. I had fucked plenty of guys, but Cash made me feel like a blushing virgin. I shook my head to clear it and dropped to my knees in front of him. The warm water rained down on me as I smiled up at him. I wanted to show him just how good I could make him feel, and I reached out and grasped his large cock in my hand. I stroked it hard, running the tip of my thumb over the head until a drop of precum oozed out. I licked it away, and he inhaled sharply at the feel of my warm tongue.

Still looking up at him, I took the head of his cock into my mouth and suckled hard on it. His hands threaded through my hair, and he gripped me firmly as I slid more of his cock into my mouth. It was so thick and long that I only got about halfway down before I had to stop. I took a deep breath and relaxed my throat. I was determined to take all of him. I took another couple of inches before I had to stop. I grunted in disappointment and took the base of him in my hand, twisting gently as I sucked him off with firm strokes of my mouth.

He thrust his hips back and forth, fucking my mouth with his cock as I sucked and squeezed and rubbed. After a few minutes, he pulled me off his cock and lifted me to my feet. I moaned in disappointment, and he kissed me hard on the mouth.

"You're going to make me come if you keep doing that," he said.

I shivered in delight and squeezed his cock with my hand, forcing a low groan from his throat. "I like it when you come."

He led me from the shower and quickly dried me off with a towel before running it over his own damp body. He lifted me and carried me to his bed, dropping me on my hands and knees.

"Don't move, little lamb," he instructed as he reached for a condom. I wiggled my ass at him and winked at him over my shoulder.

He laughed and slapped my bare ass, making me squeal. He rolled the condom on and positioned his large body behind mine. He placed his cock at the entrance to my pussy and shoved it in with one hard thrust. I cried out at the familiar feel of his hard cock stretching my pussy to the limits and braced my hands on the bed as he rocked my small body back and forth.

I reached between my legs and rubbed my hard and swollen button as he pounded into my pussy. I rubbed furiously, my legs shaking and my hair hanging in my face as I moaned and shook beneath him.

His hands suddenly tightened on my hips, and he shouted

before slamming into me one final time. I gave my own cry and raked my fingers across my clit, shuddering as my orgasm raced through my body. He fell forward, and I collapsed under his weight. His harsh breath stirred my wet hair, and I turned my head and kissed him on the cheek.

"Thank you."

"My pleasure, little lamb." He rolled off of me, and we climbed under the covers. I snuggled up to him, putting my arm around his waist and resting my cheek against his chest.

"Are you hungry?"

"A little but more tired." I sighed contentedly and closed my eyes as he rubbed my back with his warm hand.

CHAPTER 5

"Little lamb, I want you to move in with us."

I looked up from the armchair in Cash's office. It was Sunday afternoon, and I was curled up in the chair under a blanket, leafing through one of the books from his library and trying to work up my courage to call my mother for bus money.

"What?" I sputtered and dropped the book on the floor. Cash stared at me calmly from his office chair.

"I said I want you to move in with us."

"I – Cash, that's really nice of you, but…"

"But what?"

"Have you talked to Jesse about me moving in?"

"This is my home and I decide who lives here and who doesn't," he said. "Although I have spoken to Jesse and he's fine with it."

"Cash, it's really nice of you to offer, but I don't need your pity."

He frowned and crossed the room to kneel at the foot of my chair. He unfolded the blanket that I had wrapped around myself. I was wearing his t-shirt again, and he slid his hands up my bare legs to rub my thighs.

"It's not pity, Del. I like you. I want you to move in with me. You'll be paying rent and chipping in for food."

He pushed his shirt up around my waist, parted my legs and dipped his head between my pale thighs, licking lightly at my pussy lips.

I pushed his head away, glancing nervously at the open door of his office. "Don't, Cash. Jesse could walk by."

He frowned at me and squeezed my thighs firmly. "Spread your legs, Del."

I shook my head. "No."

His nostrils flared. "If you don't do what I'm telling you to do, not only will I put you over my knee and spank your bare ass, I'll invite Jesse in to watch as I do it."

He meant every word. I could see it in his cool gaze. Even as my mind balked at being treated like a child, my pussy pulsed and wetness dripped down my thigh.

"Last chance, Del." He suddenly slapped the top of my thigh, hard enough to leave a red mark. I gasped and hooked my legs over the arms of the chair, spreading my pussy wide for him.

He traced the wetness on my thigh. "You like being told what to do."

"No, I don't," I protested as he licked the cream from my skin.

"Yes, you do." He flicked his tongue against my clit, and I squealed with pleasure.

"I can't afford rent at this place," I squeaked out. If my shit-ass apartment cost nine hundred a month, I could only imagine what a third of the rent cost for a place like this.

"I think you'll find rent here to be very reasonable." Cash grinned before delving back into my dripping pussy like a honeybee in a flower.

"How does three hundred a month sound?" He asked before probing his tongue deep inside of me.

I twisted my fingers in his hair and moaned, "Too low."

"Too low? How's this?" He moved back up to my clit and flicked it with his delightfully warm tongue.

I moaned again and arched my hips. "No, I mean the rent is too low."

He laughed, his mouth vibrating against me, and I twitched in pleasure. "You can take the guest bedroom, or you can move into my bedroom with me. I'll confess that I would prefer it if you stayed in my bedroom. It's much easier to fuck you in the middle of the night if you're in my bed."

He sucked on my clit, and I thrust my hips against his face. He glanced up at me, his mouth and dark stubble soaked and shiny with my juices. "Say yes, little lamb."

"Cash I -"

"Hey, Cash? Have you talked -"

Jesse stuck his head into the library, and I shrieked and jerked against Cash's mouth.

"Woops! Sorry!" Jesse laughed and ducked back out of the room.

"Let me go!" I tried to wiggle away from his mouth, and Cash growled and yanked me back toward him.

"Have I talked about what?" he called over his shoulder before diving back into my soaking muff.

"Talked to Del about moving in," Jesse said.

"Oh my God," I moaned. "Cash, stop this right now!"

"Stop what? This?" He licked my clit with long, firm strokes, and I was helpless to stop the loud moan from escaping my lips. I clamped my hand over my mouth as Jesse laughed in the hallway.

"I was just discussing it with her right now." Cash stuck one thick finger deep into my pussy.

"What's your answer, little lamb?" He laved at my clit

again as I twisted and squirmed. I wondered if Jesse was touching himself in the hallway. Wondered if he had gotten a good look at my pussy and if he thought it was as pretty as Cash did. I groaned behind my hand. I was so fucking turned on, I was seconds away from coming all over Cash's face.

I couldn't believe this was happening. Jesse was standing outside the door, listening as Cash ate my pussy, and it was the hottest goddamn moment of my life.

"Yes or no?" Cash's voice was muffled. As he thrust another thick finger inside of me and flicked my clit rapidly with his tongue, I closed my eyes and arched my back, dropping the hand that was over my mouth onto the top of Cash's head as he brought me to a body-shuddering orgasm with his lips and tongue.

"Yesssss!" I cried, my hips pumping against Cash's face before I collapsed into the chair. My eyes fluttered open, and I checked the doorway. It was empty, and my behaviour suddenly mortified me. I had just come loudly while Jesse stood in the hallway and listened.

Cash grinned up at me and wiped his face on my pale thigh. "She said yes, Jesse."

Jesse laughed. "Yeah, I caught that. I'm going to go start lunch." His footsteps faded down the hall.

"THIS IS YOUR CAR?"

Cash and I were standing in the parking lot of my apartment building, and he eyed my car with distaste.

"Yes," I said as I pulled out my phone.

"What are you doing?"

"Looking up the number of a tow company. I'll get it towed to a mechanic and -"

"I don't think there's much point."

I frowned at him. "I can't leave it here, and I need a car."

He shook his head. "No, you don't. You can borrow my car whenever you need it."

"No, that's okay," I said.

Now it was his turn to frown. "Let's put this a different way, Del – this car is a dangerous piece of crap and I don't like the idea of you driving it."

"It's not that bad," I said.

He just stared at me, and I sighed. "I know, but it's my car and I need it."

"You really don't," he said. "You told me you take the bus to work anyway, and you can use my car for any errands you want to do. Besides," he continued, "I think this piece of junk is going to need more repairs than you can afford."

He was right, and I nodded in defeat. "Yeah, you're right. But I still need to get it towed to a junk yard or something. I can't leave it here."

"I'll take care of it," Cash said. "C'mon, let's get your stuff."

"I don't think this is a good idea, Cash," I said as we walked to the front of my apartment.

"As much as I enjoy watching you walking around my apartment in nothing but my t-shirt, you need your stuff, Del."

"It's just clothes. I'll buy some more."

"You don't have any other personal stuff that you want?"

"A few things, I guess." I followed him up the stairs, tugging my work skirt down.

"Which apartment is the landlord's?"

"Five," I said.

He buzzed the apartment and waited patiently.

"Yeah?" Todd's voice came through the speaker, tinny and disinterested.

"Hello. I'm -" Cash paused and looked at me. "What's your last name?"

"Ford."

"I'm Ms. Ford's lawyer, and I'm here to discuss the matter of her personal items in her apartment."

"That bitch don't live here no more," Todd said.

"I'm well aware of that. We're here to pick up her things. I suggest you let us in and meet us at Ms. Ford's apartment so she can gather her stuff. Unless you want to be sued for violating the rental agreement."

Cash smiled at me and waited calmly. After a few moments, the buzzer sounded, and the front door clicked open. He opened the door and held out his arm. "After you, little lamb."

Todd was waiting at my apartment door, and he stared suspiciously at Cash. "You don't look like no lawyer."

Cash glanced at his jeans and t-shirt before giving Todd a cold look. "Shut up and open the goddamn door."

Todd took a step back and stared nervously down the empty hallway. I didn't blame him. Cash towered over him and outweighed him by fifty pounds. After giving me a sullen look, Todd took a ring of keys from his pocket and opened the door.

I slipped into the apartment, Cash following closely behind me. "You can wait out here." He closed the door in Todd's face and glanced around.

My face flaming with embarrassment at the tiny, ugly apartment, I pulled my suitcase out of the closet and ran to the dresser beside my small bed. I threw my pitiful amount of clothes into the suitcase and scurried into the bathroom to gather my toiletries.

Cash studied the apartment with disgust. "How long have you been living here, Del?"

I looked up from grabbing some photos off the top of the dresser. "Almost a year."

"Jesus Christ." He looked out the window, his face wrinkling in distaste. "I think there's a dead man in the alley."

I joined him at the window. "Nope, that's Tony. He lives there."

Cash shook his head. "I can't believe you haven't been raped or murdered."

"I have mace."

He shook his head again as the sound of the opening credits to *Golden Girls* drifted through the wall. My eyes widened, and I hurriedly zipped my suitcase. I had to get him out of here before Jerry started masturbating and calling Bea's name.

"Okay, I'm ready." I lugged my suitcase to the floor.

He took another look around. "Are you sure? Do you have everything? I'm not letting you set foot in this place again, little lamb."

"Yes, yes." I dragged my suitcase toward the door, and Cash picked it up and carried it across the small apartment.

"Oh, Bea, oh God, Bea..."

Jerry's raspy voice came through the wall loud and clear, as did the unmistakable sounds of someone whacking off.

Cash arched his eyebrow at me, and I managed a weak smile. "That's just Jerry. He uh – he really likes the *Golden Girls*."

"I can tell." He held out his hand, and I took it, letting him lead me to the door of the apartment. He opened it and stepped into the hallway, glaring at Todd.

Todd stared sullenly at him. "That bitch still owes me rent."

Cash dropped my suitcase and my hand and slammed Todd up against the wall so hard that Jerry's moans cut out. "Her name is Ms. Ford, not bitch. If you ever try to contact her again, I'll rip your spine out through your mouth. Do you understand?"

Todd nodded, his eyes wide with fear, and Cash smiled. "Excellent. Have a good day."

"How old are you, Del?" Cash asked as we drove back to his apartment.

"I'm twenty-five. How old are you?"

"Thirty-five." He glanced at me. "Does that bother you?"

I shook my head. "No. You've got pretty good stamina for an old man."

He laughed and squeezed my bare thigh. "Thanks."

"What's your first name?" It was an incredibly stupid question considering that I had fucked him a few times now.

"Henry."

"I see why you go by Cash," I said.

He growled and squeezed my leg again. "Someone's looking for a spanking."

A ripple of pleasure went through me. I had dated a guy for a few months who liked to be tied up, gagged, and spanked. He even bought me a leather outfit to wear and a riding crop to use on him. I once spent an entire Saturday afternoon leading him around his apartment on a collar and leash, barking out orders at him like a Marine sergeant. But being a dominatrix wasn't really my thing. I liked the idea of being the spankee more than the spanker. I had asked him to spank me, and when he balked at it, I took that as my cue to leave.

Now, as a vision of Cash spanking me flooded through my head, I could feel my panty-less pussy growing wet. I squirmed a little on the seat. I had to think of something else quickly before I made a mess on Cash's car seat.

Cash grinned at my flushed face. "I think you like that idea."

"No, I don't."

I don't know why I lied.

He stopped at a red light. He reached between my legs and cupped my pussy. His fingers slid easily through the wetness and into my velvet warmth. I gave a little moan as he grinned at me.

"Liar."

I clutched his arm and rubbed my pussy against him. He rewarded me with a few strokes of my clit before pulling his hand free. As the light turned green, he stepped on the gas and stuck his finger in his mouth, licking it clean.

"You are so delightful, Del." He grinned at me. "So sweet and innocent."

I laughed. "I'm not innocent, Cash."

"How did you end up working at the bar?"

I shrugged. "It was the only job I could get when I moved to the city."

"Why did you move to the city?"

"I was tired of living in my parents' basement." I was starting to get uncomfortable. I hated answering questions about my loser life.

"Did you go to college?" Cash asked.

"For a while. I left after only a year because it wasn't really for me." I decided not to tell him that I was caught fucking my English professor.

Before he could ask me another question, I asked him one. "How did you get so rich?"

He laughed. "A lot of hard work and sacrifice."

"Do you like your job?"

He nodded. "I do. It gives me the opportunity to do a lot of things I wouldn't otherwise get to do."

"Like offering charity to broke bar waitresses?" I asked.

He grinned at me. "It's not charity – you're paying rent, remember."

"Speaking of which," I took a deep breath, "what's the deal with me living with you anyway? Is my length of stay determined by how often I have sex with you?"

He stared admiringly at me. "You're very blunt, aren't you?"

"Just want to know the rules."

"As I said earlier, you can move into the guest room if you'd like. Living at the apartment isn't contingent on having sex with me. Although I hope you'll consider having sex with me on a regular basis. We do seem to be," he paused, "compatible."

I burst out laughing. "Christ, that's romantic."

"Hey, you started this, little lamb," he said with a grin. "Here's the deal – I'm not good at relationships, never have been, never will be. I'm not looking for a conventional relationship with you, but I would like to enjoy your company. If you're not into that, you can still live at the apartment for as long as you need or want to. I won't ask you for anything other than rent money."

I hesitated. There was something I wanted to know, but I wasn't sure how to ask. I decided just to say it.

"Are you a Dom?"

He smiled a little and seemed to choose his words carefully. "Not exactly. Although I do expect a certain type of obedience when you're in my bed."

I frowned. I wasn't one for blind obedience.

"I do have some items that I like my woman to wear and use in bed," he admitted. "I'm drawn to women who are naturally submissive."

That made me laugh. "I'm not submissive, Cash."

He arched his eyebrow at me. "Maybe outside of the bedroom you aren't, but in bed you definitely are. You just need someone to guide you."

"I don't like being told what to do," I said.

"Are you sure about that, little lamb?" His big hand came down on my bare thigh and kneaded gently. "Earlier in my office, you were very quick to obey me. You did exactly what I told you to do, even knowing that Jesse was in the hallway listening to me eat your sweet pussy."

I blushed, and he laughed and slipped his hand under my skirt to stroke my inner thigh. "It's nothing to be ashamed of, Del."

His thumb rubbed the sensitive skin of my thigh. "Like I said before, if you're not into any of this, I won't kick you out of the apartment. I want to be upfront with you about what I expect from you in bed. You'll do what I tell you to do, or there will be consequences."

"No, you're not a Dom at all," I said.

"I'm not a true Dom, sweet lamb. I like to think of it as having Dom tendencies. If you'd like, I can take you to certain nightclubs that will show you what a true Dom is."

He squeezed my thigh again. "Don't feel any pressure about this, Del. I give you my word that if you're not into it or if at any time you decide you don't want to keep fucking me, I will not kick you out of the apartment."

"And if I am into it?"

He smiled. "Then there are, as a matter of fact, a few rules. One – exclusivity. As long as you're sleeping with me, you're not fucking anyone else. Two – we both get tested for diseases and then share the results. I hate wearing condoms. Three – you submit to me in bed and agree to accept the consequences if you don't, and four - you don't fall in love with me."

I laughed. "God, you're an arrogant bastard, aren't you?"

"Just want to make the rules clear, Del."

"Will you be following rule one as well?"

"Yes."

I shifted in my seat to face him. "Then I'm in." I held out my hand and wiggled my eyebrows at him.

He hesitated and then shook my hand. "Remember, little lamb – don't fall in love with me. There's a reason I'm still single at my age."

I smiled cheekily at him. "Don't you go fallin' in love with me, Mr. Cash. I'll break your heart."

CHAPTER 6

I settled back into the car seat. I had a vague feeling like I had just made a deal with the devil, but my dripping pussy had overridden my hesitation. I had to admit, the submission thing made me curious. My previous lovers were all too eager to do what I wanted. I wasn't exactly bossy in bed, but I had grown used to being the one in control. What exactly would it be like not to have that control? I'd gotten a taste of it in his office this morning, and I was lying if I said I didn't enjoy it.

Still, I couldn't quite wrap my head around the thought of giving up complete control. Of doing exactly what Cash told me to do without question. I was about to find out.

Lost in my thoughts, I looked around in surprise when Cash shut off the car. We were parked on a side street in a neighbourhood that boasted large lawns and immaculate flowerbeds.

"What are we doing here?" I asked as a man walking a dog passed by the car. He waved to Cash, who nodded back.

"You're going to suck my cock." He was unzipping his jeans, and I gave him a look of alarm.

"I can't! Not here – people are walking by."

"There was. He's gone," he corrected me.

"Cash, it's the middle of the afternoon. If anyone walks by, they'll…"

"See you sucking my cock?"

"Yes!"

"You agreed to this. Rule three, remember, Del?" he said. He had his cock out now and was stroking it back and forth with one large hand.

"We're not in bed," I said.

He just stared at me and continued to stroke his cock. I tried to keep my eyes away from his crotch, but couldn't. I stared at the drop of precum at the tip of his cock and licked my lips. He laughed smugly, and I glared at him.

"Now, Del," he said. "I won't ask you again."

Snorting angrily, I unlocked my seat belt, scooted to the edge of my seat and leaned over. I grimaced as the gear stick dug into my stomach, but Cash's large hand was now on my back, and I was pinned in the position.

"Go on, Del. Suck my cock with that beautiful wet mouth," he demanded.

I slid my lips down over his cock. He pushed on the back of my head, and I opened my mouth wide as his thick, hard cock filled my mouth. I sucked firmly on it as he swept my hair back from my face.

"That's my good girl." His thumb stroked my temple. "You look so good with my cock in your mouth."

I moaned around his cock, my lips vibrating against his hard shaft, and he shuddered all over.

"Faster," he demanded.

I sucked on just the head, pumping the rest of his shaft with my hand as his hips rose off the seat. His hand tightened in my hair until it pulled tightly, and I made a whimper of pain.

He pulled me away from the head of his cock and stared at my swollen and red mouth. "I said to suck my cock, Del, not give me a hand job."

"It's too big," I complained.

He rubbed his thumb over my bottom lip. "It will get easier each time."

"I don't know about that," I said.

He grinned wickedly. "It just means you'll be practicing every night."

A shudder of desire went through me as he pushed my head back toward his cock. I parted my lips obediently and took his cock into my mouth until the crown of it hit the back of my throat. I choked a little and, with my eyes watering, moved my head back until I was sucking on half of it.

"You're doing very well, little lamb. In no time at all, you'll have my entire cock in your mouth." He petted my long hair like I was a cat as his other hand dug into the pocket of his jeans.

He tugged on my hair, and I pulled my mouth free. I started to sit up, and he pressed on my back and handed me the condom. "Put this on me."

I did what he asked. My hands were shaking so badly from excitement and desire that I was afraid I would rip the thin rubber.

He waited patiently as I smoothed it on and then pushed the seat lever to move his seat back. He patted his lap. "Climb on."

I looked through the windshield nervously. A few blocks down the street, I could see the man and his dog walking back toward us. "Cash, the guy is coming back."

He sighed irritably. "I don't care. Get your sweet ass over here, Del, or the guy's going to see you getting fucked over the hood of my car."

I squirmed my way past the gear shift, cursing when it

dug into my thigh and straddled his lap. He wormed my skirt upward until cool air stirred across my naked ass and pussy. He put his hands on my hips and lowered me down until I could feel his cock against my wet slit.

"Oh God," I whimpered as he rubbed it back and forth over my clit. "Cash, please hurry."

I looked behind me to see how close the man and his dog were. Immediately, Cash's hands were in my hair, and he was yanking my face back to his.

"Look at me and only me when I'm fucking you," he said.

He pushed his cock deep into my pussy. I was so wet there was no resistance at all, and he grinned smugly. "I knew you were submissive."

He kissed me before I could argue. I moaned into his mouth and sucked eagerly on his tongue when he thrust it into my mouth. He was moving slowly inside of me, and I had forgotten entirely about the dog walker. Hell, even if I had remembered, I wouldn't have cared. Nothing mattered to me now but being fucked by Cash.

His hands moved to my breasts, and then he was pulling the neckline of my t-shirt and the cups of my bra down until my heavy breasts spilled out.

"If you had been a good girl," he panted against my mouth, "and done exactly what I told you to do, I would have allowed you to keep your shirt on. But since you insisted on questioning me…"

He flicked lazily at my left nipple, and I cried out at the combination of pain and pleasure. "Now, if anyone does walk by, they're going to get an eyeful of your gorgeous tits."

He cupped my ass and rammed in and out. My breasts bounced and I clutched at his shoulders, riding him help-lessly as he fucked me hard.

"Don't come yet," he said.

"I need to," I whimpered.

He slapped my bare ass, and I jerked at the stinging pain.

"Don't you dare," he warned before sucking hard on my bottom lip.

He reached between us and rubbed his fingers over my clit. I nearly came all over his fingers, but controlled myself grimly.

"Please, Cash. Please." I didn't recognize my own voice pleading and whimpering the way it was.

"Do you want to come, little lamb?" His deep voice whispered in my ear as he continued to stroke my clit, his cock slowing down to a gentle thrusting motion.

"Yes, yes, yes," I moaned repeatedly.

He leaned back. His eyes took in my red mouth, my swollen and rock hard nipples, and the pleading look on my face. He rubbed at my clit once more, and I almost bucked my way free of his lap. He held me steady with one strong hand around the back of my neck. His fingers circled and rubbed my clit as I closed my eyes and silently begged for mercy. I was going to come, I knew I was going to, and I didn't know what Cash would do to me when I did.

"Come for me, Del. Come, right now," he growled in my ear and then pinched my clit.

With a scream of pleasure, I arched my back and came violently around him. Dimly, I was aware of him finding his own release, of his hot breath panting in my ear and his hips arching into mine. I collapsed against his hard chest, breathing harshly and whimpering in complaint when he pushed me back.

"Shh, little lamb," he soothed as he tucked my breasts into my bra and pulled my shirt back up. Moving quickly, he tugged down my skirt and lifted me off his lap. My head smacked the top of the car, and he winced.

"Sorry, Del."

He sat me in my seat and pulled off the condom, tying it

hurriedly and dropping it behind his seat before zipping up his pants. Only a few minutes later, the man and his dog walked by the car. He waved again to Cash, and Cash returned his wave before starting the car.

"Seatbelt, Del."

Moving slowly, I clicked my seatbelt into place as Cash pulled into the street. I let my head rest against the back of the seat and stared dreamily out the window. After a few minutes, Cash put his hand on my leg. "Are you okay?"

I wondered if I was imagining the tinge of worry in his voice. I turned my head and smiled at him. "I'm fucking fantastic. How are you?"

He laughed. "I'm very pleased with my little lamb. I think we're going to get along extremely well."

I felt a rush of warmth at his words, and my pussy tingled pleasantly. I was tired, my thighs ached from straddling his large body, and I would probably have a bruise on my stomach from the gear shift, but Cash had just given me the biggest orgasm of my life.

As he started towards his home - our home now - I felt a thin thread of worry. I still wasn't entirely sure that I was as submissive as Cash said I was. I wondered what would happen the first time I balked at one of his commands.

As if sensing my worry, his hand curled into mine, and he squeezed gently. I squeezed back before staring out the window. It would be fine. I wouldn't have to do anything I didn't want to, and I knew without a doubt that Cash would never hurt me.

CHAPTER 7

"Sweet Jesus! Christ, that fucking hurts!"

I hung my jacket on the coat rack before hurrying into the kitchen. I set the bags of groceries down as another cry of pain came from the hallway.

I knocked on Jesse's open bedroom door. "Jesse? Are you okay?"

I had been living in the apartment for nearly three weeks. Truth be told, it still felt a little weird to know that after work, instead of going home to the sound of an old man masturbating to *Golden Girl* reruns, I would be going home to a home-cooked meal. Jesse was a fantastic cook. I'd probably gained five pounds alone in the last three weeks, and it would have been more if I didn't burn so many calories in Cash's bed.

Jesse and Cash were close, and it was easy to see that despite their differences, they respected and liked each other a great deal. I thought it might have felt strange to live with both of them, but it was actually kind of nice.

Although Cash rarely went to the office on the weekends, he worked long hours during the week. On the nights that I wasn't working at the bar, Jesse would keep me amused with stories of his gigs and the women who hit on him until Cash came home. The three of us would eat a late dinner together and chat about our day.

Jesse surprised me a little. If he brought women home, we never saw them, and he didn't live the lifestyle of a rock star. He rarely drank, didn't smoke, and this was one of the few times I had heard him swear.

I knocked again as another string of curses drifted toward me. "Jesse? Can I come in?"

"Yeah," he grunted, and I slipped inside.

I had never been in his bedroom before, and I was a little surprised at how tidy and clean it was. He really wasn't anything like I thought.

"Jesse?"

"In here."

I followed his voice to the small bathroom off the bedroom.

"What the hell are you doing?" I would have laughed if Jesse hadn't looked so miserable.

"What does it look like I'm doing, Del?" he said grumpily.

He was standing at the sink wearing just a pair of boxers. A bowl of wax with a wooden stick stuck in the middle of it was balanced carefully on the sink. There were pieces of long, white fabric covered in wax and hair littered on the floor. His chest was covered in bits of fabric and wax, with a strip of fabric glued to it. He was gripping the edge of it and already wincing.

"Why are you waxing your own chest, Jesse?" I leaned against the doorway and swallowed down my laughter.

"Because I couldn't get in to see my regular girl, and I have a gig tomorrow night. I figured it couldn't be that difficult," he said through gritted teeth. His hands continued to hold the edge of the fabric, but I sensed he was trying to work up his nerve.

"Yeah, you don't seem to be having any trouble at all." I giggled.

"This isn't funny, Del. Christ, why does it hurt so much? It doesn't hurt this much when Tawny does it."

"Tawny?" I rolled my eyes and stepped into the bathroom. "Here, let me."

He took a step back. "Have you done this before?"

I rolled my eyes again and hoisted up my leg to rest my foot on the sink. "My legs don't get this smooth from shaving, buddy. Unlike you, I can't afford to have someone named Tawny wax the hair off my body."

He reached out and ran his hand over my shin. I shook off the beat of pleasure I felt at his touch and dropped my leg back to the floor. I pushed his hand out of the way and grabbed the strip of fabric. "Ready?"

He stiffened. "Yeah, do it."

I rested my hand on his chest, stretching the skin a bit, and tore the strip off with a short, hard tug. He winced in pain, and I glanced at the strip. "Christ, Jesse, you're using way too much wax."

He had waxed half of his chest, and the skin was red and angry looking. Sighing, I picked up the bowl of wax and the rest of the clean strips.

"Come with me."

He followed me into the bedroom, and I pointed at the bed. "Lie down."

He obeyed, and I set the bowl of wax on his bedside table. "I don't know why you wax your chest anyway. You've got blond hair and not even that much." It was Cash's chest I was thinking of, the thick mat of dark curly hair that covered it. I loved running my fingers through it.

He shrugged and put his hands behind his head as I used

the flat stick to apply a thin layer of wax to the hair on his chest. "The girls prefer a smooth chest."

"Not all of us." I smoothed the fabric down and, with another short, hard tug, pulled it free.

"Hey, you're not half bad at this," he said admiringly. "That hardly hurt."

I applied another thin layer of wax. "It's all in the technique, my friend."

In less than ten minutes, I had removed all of the hair on his chest. "How's that?"

He looked down. "It's good. Thank you, Del."

"You're welcome."

He ran his fingers across the thin trail of hair below his navel. "What do you think? Do I get rid of this? I normally do."

I shook my head. "No, don't." I watched his long fingers brush over his abdomen as heat rushed to my cheeks.

"All right." He smiled at me, and I forced myself to look back at his chest.

"Hold on a minute, Jesse."

I walked to the bathroom and returned with a warm, wet cloth and a towel. Carefully, I wiped the bits of fabric from his chest. He hissed in pain when I scrubbed at the wax that still clung to his chest.

He stared ruefully at the red, swollen skin. "Looks like I'm going to be keeping my shirt on tomorrow night. All that pain for nothing."

I shrugged. "Maybe not. Do you have any aloe vera cream?"

"Yeah."

I stood to go back to the bathroom, and he grabbed my hand. "No, it's here."

He reached into the drawer of the nightstand and brought out the bottle of lotion. I stared at it for a moment before taking it from him. A hot blush was rising in my cheeks as I thought about all the reasons why he would have the bottle of lotion next to his bed. When I finally raised my gaze to his, the look on his face suggested he knew exactly what I was thinking, and my blush deepened.

He grinned boyishly at me and put his hands under his head again. I squirted some lotion onto my hands and gently rubbed it into his skin. His back arched the tiniest bit, and he bit his lip.

"I'm sorry, does that hurt?" I said, my hands pausing above his chest.

"No, it feels really good," he said hoarsely.

I cleared my throat and continued to smooth the cream into his skin. My fingers brushed across one of his nipple rings, and he inhaled sharply.

"Sorry."

He didn't reply, and I searched for something to say. "Did it hurt to get the piercings?"

"A little. The waxing hurts worse," he said.

I continued to rub the lotion into his chest. I didn't need to. There was more than enough to help heal and soothe his skin, but I couldn't seem to stop touching him. He was smaller and more compact than Cash. Although Cash had an obvious six-pack, Jesse's chest and abdomen were like sculpted glass.

There was a gym in the apartment building, and both Jesse and Cash went to it daily. I went a couple of times with Cash and hated every minute of it. Of course, if I kept eating Jesse's food the way I was, I'd have to suck it up and go every day like they did.

I realized with a start that while I was thinking of the gym, my hand had wandered down to Jesse's abdomen, and I was tracing the hard muscles with the tips of my fingers. His breathing was ragged, and I snatched my hand back, my face so red it felt like it was on fire.

I took a glance at his crotch. His erection was obvious through the thin boxers, and I stood up and stumbled away from the bed. I couldn't look at him.

"Uh, I should go and put the groceries away," I mumbled before fleeing his room.

I ran to the kitchen and leaned against the fridge, resting my hot forehead against the cool steel. My nipples were hard and rubbing against my bra, and I wanted to stick my hand down my jeans and rub my clit. It would be wet and swollen and –

"Del? Are you okay?"

I whipped around and stared at Jesse. He'd put on a pair of jeans but left his upper body bare, and I stared at his glistening chest. Christ, I wanted him badly.

He frowned and moved toward me before cupping my head. "Del? What's wrong?"

"Nothing." My eyes dropped to his mouth. He had a gorgeous mouth – full, firm lips that would taste delicious.

An image of those lips sucking on my throbbing nipples went through my head, and I clamped my mouth shut around the groan that wanted to break free of my throat. As if he read my mind, his gaze fell on my tits. My nipples were so hard they were clearly visible even through my shirt and bra, and I felt, more than heard, his intake of breath.

His hand left my head and drifted down my arm, cupping and squeezing my biceps. His thumb was inching towards my right nipple when I finally came to my senses. I squeezed past him and ran for the kitchen door.

"I'm sorry, Jesse," I tossed back over my shoulder. "I'm not feeling very well. I think I'll go to bed."

"WHAT'S GOTTEN INTO YOU, LITTLE LAMB?" CASH RUMBLED below me. I was riding him furiously, my entire body aching and throbbing for release as his large hands massaged and kneaded my tits.

"Nothing," I panted. I couldn't tell him the truth. I couldn't tell him that I spent most of the evening waiting frantically for him to get home so that I could fuck his brains out. I couldn't tell him that I suddenly wanted Jesse as badly as I wanted him.

I reached down and rubbed my clit as I rode Cash's hard cock. He pulled my hand away. "No, not yet, Del."

I shook free of his grip and moved my hand back to my clit. Cash had been dominant in bed the last three weeks, often dictating what positions he wanted me in and when I could come, but it hadn't gone much beyond that. I didn't think about it much; I just assumed that since I did everything he asked, he didn't feel the need to go any further.

Tonight, I felt different. Tonight, I needed to come, and I would be damned if he told me I couldn't.

"Del," he growled warningly, "don't come."

I ignored him and rubbed harder. I was already so close, and Cash's thick cock was working its usual magic in my pussy. Before he could pull my hand away, I pinched my clit and arched my back, groaning with pleasure as I climaxed around his thick cock. My pussy squeezed his cock, and he cursed under his breath, his hips arching involuntarily under me.

Panting, I collapsed against his broad chest and gave myself a moment to catch my breath. He was still hard inside of me, and I sat up and smiled at him.

"Your turn," I purred.

He was staring at me sternly, and I had time for one small squeak before he pushed me off of him. I fell back on the bed, and he hovered over me, his face dark with disapproval.

"What did I tell you, Del?" he said.

I stared at him, feeling both fear and lust tingling through my veins. "Cash I -"

"What did I tell you?"

"I needed to come. I was going to lose it if I didn't." I tried to joke with him.

"I made it very clear that I expect obedience in my bed," his hand tangled in my hair and pulled lightly, "and if you didn't obey me there would be consequences."

He kissed my mouth. "Do you remember that conversation?"

"Yes," I whispered.

"Yet you defied me tonight." He traced my lips with his finger, and when he probed at them, I opened my mouth so he could slide it between my lips. I sucked on his finger as he pressed his erection against my hip.

"Now you have to pay the price for your defiance." He sucked my earlobe into his mouth, and I moaned around his finger.

He sat up, and before I could react, yanked me over his lap. My bare ass stuck up in the air, and I squealed and struggled as he clamped a hard arm over my back.

"Stop moving," he said.

I ignored him and continued to wiggle. I shrieked in surprise at the first hard slap on my bare ass. It burned like fire and shocked me into stillness.

His hand stroked my lower back. "Such a lovely ass you have, Del." He stroked and kneaded the warm flesh. "I've wanted to spank it since the first night I saw you in the bar."

"Cash, please," I pleaded, turning my head to look at him. "I'm sorry. I won't do it again."

"I know." He gave me a warm and gentle smile and then slapped my ass hard once again.

I squealed, and tears came to my eyes. Christ, it hurt! His

hand soothed my throbbing skin for a moment before he slapped it again.

I moaned and twisted and struggled as he spanked me slowly and methodically. I punched at him with wildly swinging fists. He grabbed my wrists in one hard hand and held them behind my back. He raised his legs so my ass was even higher and continued to spank until my ass was a fiery red and tears were coursing down my cheeks. It was only when I had given up struggling, when I had submitted to his strength and lay weakly on his lap, that he stopped.

He dipped his hand between my legs. I was surprised to realize that I was soaking wet. My pussy was dripping, and my inner thighs were drenched in moisture. He slid his finger into my pussy, and I moaned with pleasure, even as my ass continued to burn. He ran his finger over my clit, and I jerked against his lap, another soft cry escaping my throat.

"Get on your hands and knees, Del." He lifted me off his lap, and I immediately scrambled to obey him. I knelt on my hands and knees, spreading my legs wide.

"Good girl." He pushed between my thighs, his large ones stretching them apart even further and rubbed the head of his cock against my dripping slit. "Are you going to disobey me again, little lamb?"

"No." I shook my head. "I won't. I promise, Cash."

He tangled his hand in my hair and pulled. My back arched, and I stared up at the ceiling as he reached around with his other hand and fondled my tit. His fingers pinched my nipple, and I moaned with pleasure. He pinched it again and then moved his hand down my flat belly and into the curls between my legs. His fingers found my clit, and he rubbed it roughly as I gasped and shuddered. The hair on his thighs was chafing my sore ass, but the pleasure between my legs was quickly blotting out the throbbing of my ass.

"Don't come, Del."

"Stop!" I gasped, twisting desperately in his grip. "Please stop. I'll come if you don't."

He laughed, a rich smug sound that should have made me angry but instead made me vibrate with lust.

"You're learning quickly, little lamb."

With a sudden grunt, he released my hair and put his large hand between my shoulder blades. He pressed hard, and I collapsed into the bed, my face buried in the sheets and my ass thrust high into the air. He grabbed my waist and, with a roughness that had me crying out with undeniable pleasure, he shoved his cock deep into my pussy.

"Oh my God!" I screamed into the sheets as he fucked me with long, hard thrusts. He plunged in and out, pounding into my pussy as I moaned and writhed and squeezed the sheets in my hands.

His fingers found my clit again, and I heard his soft command. "Come, Del. Squeeze that tight pussy around my cock right now."

My ass throbbing, my pussy gushing, and my heart pounding, I buried my face deep into the sheets and came. Cash gave his own hoarse shout as my pussy clenched around him and he came deep inside of me, flooding my insides with hot wetness. I collapsed against the bed, only vaguely aware of Cash lying down beside me. He ran his hand over my ass, and I flinched a little.

"Poor little lamb," he said before turning and rummaging in the drawer of the bedside table.

I started to roll onto my back, and he stilled me with a warm hand on my back. "Stay on your stomach, Del."

I stayed where I was as he pulled a bottle out of the drawer and squeezed a clear liquid into the palm of his hand. He gently rubbed it into my ass, smoothing it over both my cheeks.

"What is that?" I mumbled.

"Something to help with the pain." He continued to rub my ass, and after only a few moments, the sting started to fade.

He put the bottle away and drew the covers over us before turning me on my side and spooning me from behind. He cupped my breast possessively and kissed the back of my shoulder.

"Better?"

"Yeah," I said sleepily. I burrowed under the covers, sighing happily as I drifted into sleep.

CHAPTER 8

My old and battered cell phone buzzed, and I grabbed for it, scanning the screen excitedly.

Hello, little lamb.

A smile crossing my face, I turned away from my mother's view and quickly texted back.

Hey, handsome.

Having fun with your parents?

If you think being lectured about growing old and alone is fun, then yeah, I guess I am.

Poor baby. Only one more day and then you're back in my arms, where you belong.

I can't wait. I miss you.

I squeezed my phone and waited anxiously for his reply.

"Who are you talking to?"

I whipped around and held my phone to my chest, covering the screen from my mother's prying eyes. "Just a friend."

"A boyfriend?" she said hopefully.

I didn't reply, and she sighed, staring at my father, who was sitting at the table. "She's going to die old and alone."

My father shrugged. "She doesn't care that we worry about her. She doesn't care that we're going to die before she gives us grandchildren."

"I'm standing right here," I scowled at my father, "and I think Angela, Mindy, and Connie have given you more than enough grandchildren."

He rolled his eyes, and my mother returned to the stove, lifting the lid on the pot of potatoes and testing them with a fork.

I leaned against the counter. I had just arrived last night, and already they were driving me crazy. I loved my parents, but I often wondered why I even bothered to visit once a month. It always ended with them lecturing me on how I needed to go back to college, how I needed to find a husband, settle down and start popping out babies.

My cell phone buzzed, and I slipped out of the kitchen, down the hallway and out the front door. I sat on the cold cement step as I shivered in the wind and glanced at the screen.

I miss you too.

I was starting to type back when he texted again.

I like your skirt, by the way.

I frowned and glanced at my navy skirt.

How did you know I was wearing a skirt? I quickly texted back, my fingers shaking from the cold.

You look like you're freezing. Why are you sitting outside in the cold?

My breath caught in my throat. I looked up to see Cash standing at the end of the sidewalk leading up to my parents' house.

I squealed like a firetruck siren and jumped up, running down the sidewalk and throwing myself at him. Laughing, he caught me and kissed me soundly on the mouth.

"What are you doing here?" I squawked.

"I told you I missed you."

"How did you know where my parents lived?"

"You told me your parents' names, and Jesse is an expert at finding people using nothing more than his laptop, an internet connection, and his wits."

I mashed my mouth down onto his. "I am so happy to see you."

"I'm happy to see you, too, little lamb." He smoothed my hair back from my face before looking up.

I followed his gaze and groaned under my breath when I realized my parents were standing on the step of the house, staring at us.

Cash dropped me gently to the ground and took my hand. "Come, little lamb. Introduce me to your parents."

He led me up the sidewalk, and I cleared my throat nervously. "Mom and Dad, this is Cash. He's my uh…"

I trailed off. Cash and I didn't have a conventional relationship, which left me unsure of what to tell my parents. Somehow, "this is the guy I live with and fuck on a daily basis" just didn't seem like the thing to say to your parents. Cash stepped forward and held out his hand.

"I'm her boyfriend," he said.

My mother's mouth dropped open, and my father reached out to take his hand, muttering an audible, "thank God," under his breath.

He shook Cash's hand. "Nice to meet you. I'm Grant, and this is my wife Debra."

My mother took his hand and stared at him. "I'm sorry, did you say your name was Cash?"

"It's Henry, actually – Henry Cash. But most people call me Cash."

"Well, it's really lovely to meet you. I'm sorry to look so shocked. Adelaide never mentioned a boyfriend."

Cash looked at me and raised his eyebrow as I flushed

under his gaze. "She didn't? Naughty Adelaide." His voice held a whispered promise that only I understood, and my pussy throbbed in hot response.

"I suppose she also hasn't mentioned that she lives with me?" Cash said.

My mother blinked in surprise. "No, she hasn't."

I groaned silently. Being strict Catholics, my parents would not take well to the news of my living in sin with a man. I waited for my mother's furious diatribe.

It didn't happen. Instead, she smiled and stepped back. "We're so glad to meet you, Mr. Cash! Please, come in, come in. Will you be staying for supper?"

Cash nodded. "I would love to if you're sure you'll have enough?"

My father laughed. "Adelaide's sisters and their families are joining us, and there will still be plenty. Trust me – my wife cooks enough for an army."

HE FOUND ME IN THE PANTRY AFTER DINNER. HE SLIPPED UP behind me and wrapped his arms around me, sliding his hands under my shirt and cupping my breasts through my bra.

I leaned against his solid warmth and smiled up at him.

"Why didn't you tell me your real name was Adelaide?" He kissed the tip of my nose.

"You never asked," I said.

He growled and squeezed my tits hard, making me gasp.

"Adelaide," he repeated, and I shivered a little at the sound of my given name rolling off his tongue. "I like it. It's pretty."

"I prefer Del," I said.

He smiled and pulled the cups of my bra down until my breasts were free. "Then I'll continue to call you Del."

"Or little lamb," I said.

"Or little lamb," he agreed and kissed me again. I sighed and opened my mouth as our tongues tangled together. His big hands were rubbing my breasts, and I pushed my ass against him when he plucked at my hard nipples.

He moved his right hand down my stomach and under the waistband of my skirt and then my panties. He cupped my hot sex, smiling approvingly at the liquid he found.

"I love how wet you are, Del," he whispered into my ear.

"You do this to me," I moaned softly as one questing finger found its way into my aching channel.

He added a second finger, and I groaned before putting my hand over his. "We need to stop."

He arched his eyebrow at me. "What did you just say?"

I flushed a little. "My parents are still in the kitchen, not to mention my eighty-seven nieces and nephews are all running around. One of them is going to come flying in here at any moment."

He chuckled. "Away from me for one night and already you've forgotten the rules." He pinched my nipple as his other hand cupped me tighter.

"The rules don't apply when we're at my parents," I said.

"The rules always apply."

He let go of my breast and took my hand. Quickly, before I could protest, he pulled it behind my back and pinned it between our bodies, using his hard abdomen to trap my hand against my back. He took my other hand as I began to struggle and jerked it between our bodies as well. He wrapped his large hand around both of my wrists and held me easily as I squirmed against him.

His fingers were still deep inside my pussy, and he watched with amusement as I wiggled and arched and tried to pull them free.

"Here's what's going to happen, sweet lamb. You're going

to spread your legs like a good girl, and I'm going to rub your clit until you come." His deep voice sent shivers down my spine.

"I can't!" I whispered. "The kitchen is right there!" I jerked my head at the far wall of the pantry.

"I know. So be very quiet when you come. You don't want your parents to hear you."

"Cash," I moaned.

He squeezed my wrists. "Spread your legs, Del. Right now. You know what will happen if you don't."

An image of Cash bending me over in the pantry and spanking me flashed through my head. I bit back the moan as my pussy gushed fresh liquid on his hand. He bit my earlobe gently, and I spread my legs as far as my skirt would let me.

"Such an obedient girl," he whispered. "Let's see how fast I can make you come."

His fingers rubbed roughly at my clit, and I clamped my mouth shut as I pressed back against him and arched my hips. He was still holding my wrists, and the thought of how I looked – hard nipples pushing against my shirt, my legs spread wide as I arched helplessly in Cash's strong grip – was enough to send me rocketing over the edge.

I gasped and shuddered soundlessly as Cash laughed softly. "It's a new record, I think, little lamb." He put his fingers in front of my mouth. "Suck."

I licked my juices from his fingers as he used his other hand to tuck my breasts back into my bra. I was breathing heavily and still leaning against him when the door to the pantry opened.

Cash turned, casually pulling me in front of him to hide his erection as Angela peeked in the small room. "There you are. Mama's looking for you."

"I'll be right out." I gave her a nervous smile as she stared at the two of us.

Cash grinned at her as he slid his arm around my waist and cupped my hip possessively. Angela blinked and then flushed a little as she suddenly realized what we were up to.

"Um, okay. I'll, uh, see you in the kitchen." She slammed the pantry door shut, and I groaned with embarrassment as Cash laughed.

"It's not funny!" I glared up at him. "She knows what we were doing in here."

"Of course she does," Cash said. "She has what – eight kids?"

"Three," I said.

He laughed. "Right – three. The twins and the baby?"

I nodded, and he kissed my forehead. "Tell me, Del, is everyone in your family this prolific?"

"Mitchell isn't married, so he doesn't have any kids yet, and Tommy and his wife just got married last year. I think they're trying, though."

"Do you want kids?"

I stared cautiously at him. "Don't tell my mother this, but no, I don't. Why?"

"I just wondered." He kissed my forehead again. "We'd better get back to your family."

He squeezed my hand and led me toward the door of the pantry.

"Cash wait – do you want kids?" I asked a bit timidly. I didn't know why, but I suddenly needed to know.

"No, little lamb. I don't."

"MY FAMILY LOVES YOU," I SAID AS CASH PUT HIS ARMS around me. I leaned back against him and sighed softly.

We were in the basement of my parents' home. They had turned my room into a sewing room for my mother, but the couch in the rec room converted into a bed. After encouraging Cash to spend the night, my mother hurriedly made the bed.

"Why do you say that?"

I laughed. "Well, for one, my parents don't have a problem with you sleeping in the same bed as me, despite not being married. Also, my mother might have pulled me aside when you were watching football with my dad and told me that I was to behave myself and hang on to you no matter what I had to do."

He laughed. "She obviously doesn't know me. I like you better when you misbehave."

I blushed a little as his hands unbuttoned my shirt. "You're quite a bit different than the men I've brought home before."

He tugged off my shirt and draped it neatly on the over-stuffed armchair. "What are they usually like?"

"Unemployed, covered in tattoos, possibly illiterate."

He laughed again, and I shushed him. "My parents' bedroom is right above us."

He unzipped my skirt, and I stepped out of it. He folded it and placed it with my shirt.

"Why did you come here tonight, Cash?" I said as he stroked my belly with his hard hands.

"You've mentioned before that your parents give you a lot of grief about not being in a relationship. I figured it would be a little easier for you if I pretended to be your adoring boyfriend."

I snickered a little. "Who knew you would do it so well?"

He pulled me back against him until his erection was pushing into my ass. "Hey, I'm not just a pretty face, you know."

"No, you're definitely not just that," I agreed breathlessly.

He left me standing in the middle of the room in my bra

and panties as he crossed the room to his overnight bag. "I have something for you, little lamb."

"What is it?"

He rifled through the bag, and my mouth dropped open when I saw the leather collar in his hand. It was thin, black in colour, with a metal loop attached to the front. A dark beat of lust pulsed deep in my belly at the sight of it. I realized he was holding something else in his right hand. Two matching leather wrist cuffs, each with its own metal loop, were dangling from his large fingers.

"Del?"

"Yeah?" My voice was hoarse.

"Will you wear them?"

"Yes."

He stood in front of me, and I lifted my hair so he could buckle the collar around my neck. He attached the leather cuffs around my thin wrists and took a step back to look at me.

"You look beautiful, Del."

"Thank you," I said.

He pulled off my bra and tugged my panties down my legs. I stepped out of them and stood quietly as he shed his clothes. His erection was massive, and my mouth started to water as I stared unabashedly at it.

"One last thing." He smiled at me and went through his bag once more. He came back with a short, thin steel chain in his hand.

"Turn around, Del."

"Cash I -"

He leaned down and kissed me. I returned his kiss, and he stroked his fingers across my face. "Trust me, little lamb. I won't hurt you. Give me a safe word."

I hesitated before saying, "Violet."

"Anytime you want to stop, just say 'violet', and I'll stop immediately, okay?"

"Okay." I took a deep breath and turned around. The chain had clasps on either end, and he brought my arms back, latching a clasp to each of the metal loops on my wrist cuffs.

"All right?"

I pulled experimentally at the cuffs. The chain held my hands behind my back, and there was no way I could free myself.

"Yes. I'm good," I said.

He turned me around and kissed me. I leaned against him, rubbing my nipples against his chest as his tongue stroked and licked at mine.

"On your knees, little lamb," he said.

He helped me drop to my knees in front of him. My mouth was directly in front of his cock, and he smiled down at me, brushing my hair back from my face.

"Open your mouth."

I opened my mouth and he guided his cock past my lips. I sucked hard on it, tasting him on my tongue as he groaned softly.

"Look at me, Del."

I raised my eyes to his obediently, and he smiled down at me. "Good. Keep sucking, slowly."

I continued to stare at him as he pushed his cock in and out of my mouth. I sucked slowly like he instructed, and a shudder of desire went through me at the look on his face. I was a little nervous. Without the use of my hands, I had no control over how much of Cash's cock I took into my mouth, but he kept a slow and steady pace and never slid more of his cock in than I could take.

"I love the way you look with that pretty mouth of yours wrapped around my cock," he said huskily.

He threaded his hands into my hair and stroked my temples with his thumbs. "You're so good at this."

He stared at me as he increased the rhythm of his hips. "Suck harder."

I did what he asked. My nipples were hard little pearls, and my pussy was throbbing with every thrust of his hips.

"Let's see how much of my thick cock you can take now, little lamb," he said.

I opened my mouth wide as he slowly pushed his cock further into my mouth. I tensed and gave him a pleading look when the head of his cock pushed at the back of my throat. He moved back slightly as I grunted with frustration and disappointment.

"Shh, little lamb," he soothed. "You're doing so well."

I tightened my lips around his smooth skin as he continued to fuck my mouth. He was starting to pant, and he made soft little groans when I used my tongue to trace around the head of his cock.

He moved with the same steady rhythm, and I had time to admire his control before his cock started to swell in my mouth. I sucked harder, bobbing my head back and forth as he moaned and his hands tightened in my hair. He pulled free of my mouth, and I whimpered in disappointment. He lifted me to my feet and kissed me sweetly.

"I want to come inside you, sweet Del."

He walked me over to the hide-a-bed and sat down on the edge of it. He patted his thighs. "Sit down."

I straddled him awkwardly with my hands still cuffed behind my back. My breasts were directly in front of his face, and he took the opportunity to suck gently on one throbbing nipple. I moaned loudly, and he grinned at me.

"Quiet, Del. Your parents are directly above us."

I gave him a mock scowl that quickly disappeared when he cupped my breasts together and ran his tongue from one nipple to the other. He bit the left one lightly, and I moaned again, rubbing my crotch against him. He lifted me with one strong arm around my waist and guided his cock into my wet opening. I let out a soft groan of need when the head of his cock slipped into my tight warmth.

"God, Del," he groaned, "you have the tightest pussy I've ever fucked."

"Please," I whispered, and he lowered me completely onto his hard cock. I made a soft noise of desire and rocked back and forth.

He groaned, and I smiled with satisfaction before whispering, "Look at me, Cash."

His eyes fluttered open, and I rocked harder as he stared into my eyes. "I love fucking you. Your cock feels so good."

He muttered something I couldn't hear and buried his face in my neck. His arms clamped around my waist like a vise and held me steady as he thrust his hips upward in short, hard movements.

I moaned and let my head fall back. My fingers clenched and unclenched as I pulled helplessly at the leather cuffs around my wrists. He kissed my neck and then pulled lightly on the collar around it with his teeth. I shuddered and twisted on top of him. My climax rushed through me, and I bit back my cry of delight as Cash thrust roughly into me and came just as quietly. His large body shivered all over, and his fingers tightened almost painfully into my soft skin before he collapsed on the bed and pulled me with him.

He reached behind me and unclasped the chain, dropping it on the floor before tucking me under the covers of the bed. He rubbed my arms lightly. "Do your arms hurt?"

I shook my head and wrapped my arms around his shoulders. "No."

He traced the collar around my neck and tugged lightly on the metal loop until I lifted my face to his. He kissed me on the mouth, sucking on my upper lip as I sighed and nestled my small body against his large one.

The bed was small and uncomfortable, but I didn't care. Snuggling into Cash's warm chest, listening to the solid beat of his heart under my ear and feeling his strong arms around me made me happier than I'd been in a long time. I closed my eyes and slept.

CHAPTER 9

I sat down at the piano in Cash's living room and traced my fingers over the ivory keys. I glanced around a bit guiltily before beginning to play. Cash and Jesse had gone downstairs to the gym five minutes ago. Like always, when I was alone in the apartment, I couldn't resist the urge to play.

I closed my eyes and let the music wash over me as my fingers floated over the keys. I played a few easier songs to warm my fingers up before playing one of Killjoy's songs. It was a rock song, but I changed it to a ballad, slowing it down and changing the key to suit my alto voice.

I finished the song, my voice echoing in the large room. Before I could start playing again, a soft voice whispered, "Holy shit."

I screamed and jerked wildly. The leather of the piano bench was slippery, and I slid off the back of it and landed on my back on the hardwood floor with a painful thump. I groaned and rubbed the back of my head as Cash's and Jesse's faces appeared above me.

They were staring at me with weird looks, and I realized my legs were still on the bench and my skirt was up around my waist. I blushed and yanked it down as Cash picked me up off the ground and set me on my feet.

"Are you okay, little lamb?" He rubbed at the knot forming on the back of my head.

"Yeah, nothing hurt but my pride," I said.

"I didn't know you played," Jesse said.

I blushed again and said, "I'm sorry I didn't ask if I could play the piano, Cash."

Cash shrugged. "This is your home too, Del. You don't have to ask my permission to play the piano."

He led me to the couch and sat down, tucking me up against him and massaging the back of my neck. I stared at my lap as Jesse collapsed in the easy chair across from us. I could feel the heat in my cheeks, and I cleared my throat nervously.

"How did you learn to play?" Jesse asked.

"Piano lessons from age five to eighteen."

"Really?"

"Yeah. My mom made all of us kids take music lessons. I can also play the violin a little, and I'm dangerous with a ukulele."

Cash laughed, and I grinned up at him. "It's true."

"You have a really great voice - very powerful," Jesse mused.

I made a face at him. "No, I don't. It's average at best."

"Did you take singing lessons as well?" Cash asked.

I shook my head and leaned against Cash as he moved his hand to my thigh and rubbed it lazily. "Nah. Not unless you count seven years in a Catholic choir as singing lessons. Weren't you two supposed to be at the gym?"

Jesse rolled his eyes. "There was another water leak. When we showed up, they were bailing it out with buckets."

We sat in comfortable silence for a few minutes, and then

Cash squeezed my leg. "Will you play something else for us, Del?"

"Oh uh," I gave him a nervous look, "I don't usually play in front of people."

"C'mon, Del. I really liked what you did to my song. Let's see what else you can do." Jesse winked at me, and I blushed for no discernible reason.

"I'd rather not." I smiled weakly at them. "I'm not that good and I -"

Cash leaned into me, his breath warm against my ear. "If you play some more for me, I'll let you come whenever and as often as you'd like tonight, little lamb," he whispered. "No rules, no limits, just you riding my cock as hard as you want to."

I shivered all over. He smiled and kissed the tip of my nose, and I grinned at him. "You're going to regret this, Cash."

"I highly doubt that, little lamb." He slapped my ass gently as I stood and walked back to the piano.

I SHIFTED THE TRAY ON MY ARM AND HANDED OUT THE margaritas to the table of women sitting closest to the stage. All their attention was trained on the stage where Jesse and the rest of Killjoy were performing. I rolled my eyes a little and patiently repeated the amount they owed until they finally shoved the money at me.

I couldn't blame them really. Jesse looked exceptionally good tonight. He was wearing a leather vest over his bare upper body and a pair of jeans that hung so low on his hips, you could see the perfectly sculpted V of his lower abdomen. I felt a tug of desire followed immediately by a feeling of guilt.

I glanced at Cash's usual table. He wasn't in the bar tonight. He had a business event to attend. No doubt he was standing in a room full of men and women who wouldn't give someone like me a second look.

I returned to the bar and leaned against it for a moment. Killjoy was on their second encore of the night, and once they finished this last song, they would call it a night. People would start leaving soon after, and I would finally get to cash out and head home. With no Cash to drive me home, Jesse had pulled me aside before taking the stage and told me he would stick around to give me a ride home.

I pushed my shoe off and rubbed my sore foot along my calf as Dana set her tray down and smiled at me. "God, I'll be glad to get off my feet. It's been busy tonight."

"It always is when Jesse plays."

She glanced appreciatively at the stage. "Christ, what I wouldn't do to have that man between my legs."

I laughed. "Yeah, you and every other woman in this bar."

"Including you?" She raised her eyebrow at me.

I shook my head. "You know I'm with Cash."

She shrugged. "Yeah, I know." Her gaze drifted to the stage again. "But I've seen the way Jesse looks at you."

I frowned at her. "What's that supposed to mean?"

"Nothing." She winked at me and goosed me lightly before strolling back to her section.

Mark handed me three beers. As Killjoy's song ended and the crowd cheered, I carried the tray across the crowded bar.

"Thank you! Thank you so much!" Jesse's voice was raspy from singing. The table of women with margaritas screamed with loud laughter when one of them stood and lifted her shirt, flashing her tits at Jesse.

"Lovely, very lovely," Jesse said into the microphone before winking at her. She giggled and shook her tits at him before the woman beside her tugged down her shirt and dragged her back into her seat.

I snorted and handed the last beer to Danny, one of the regulars.

"Thanks, Del." He smiled at me.

"You're welcome, Danny. Enjoying the show?" I looked pointedly at the flasher, and Danny grinned.

"You know it. Hey," he took my arm and squeezed it lightly before I could walk away, "I was wondering if you'd like to go out with me sometime, Del?"

I stared at him in surprise. Faintly, I could hear Jesse saying something about one last song with a special guest, but most of my attention was on Danny.

"Well, what do you think?" Danny smiled hopefully at me.

"I'm sorry, Danny. I'm already seeing someone."

"Oh," he said. "Guess I waited too long, huh?"

Before I could reply, I realized that Jesse was saying my name.

I looked up in surprise, and Jesse grinned at me. "Del? Come on up, sweetheart. We need your help for this last song."

I shook my head violently and gave him a death glare. His grin widened, and my hands tightened on the tray as he stared at the crowd.

"Ladies and gentlemen, Del seems to be a bit shy tonight. If you guys want to hear her sing with us tonight - and trust me, she's got a voice made of sin - why don't you let her know with some clapping?"

Immediately, the bar burst into applause, and I shook my head again as Danny stood and tugged the tray from my hand. "Go on, Del. Let's hear you sing."

"No!" I said sharply, but he had taken my hand and was pulling me towards the stage.

Feeling like I was hit by a very large truck, I stumbled

numbly after Danny. Jesse reached down, took my hand and led me up the three steps to the stage.

"Jesse!" I said in a low voice. "What the fuck are you doing?"

He led me to the keyboard, and their usual keyboardist, Lance, stood and ushered me onto the small leather stool. Lance smiled at me. "C'mon, Del. Jesse's been raving about your voice for two weeks now. Let's hear what you've got."

"I am going to kill you, Jesse. Do you hear me?" I said.

He laughed. "Just close your eyes and pretend you're at Cash's. It's no different than when you were singing and playing for us."

"It's completely different." I scowled at him. My hands were shaking, and I could feel my throat drying up with nervousness.

"It isn't. You'll be fine. You can do this, Del. Play our song like you did before," Jesse said.

Lance put the microphone in front of my face, and I couldn't give Jesse the very rude retort I wanted to. I settled for giving him a look that practically screamed, 'I will kill you for this, ' and placed my shaky hands on the keys.

Jesse stood next to me and squeezed my shoulder. "Just close your eyes and sing."

I closed my eyes, pictured Cash's calm face, and started playing. The crowd quieted when I began to sing. My voice sounded shaky and weak, and I straightened my body and imagined I was back in the choir at the church. Mr. Sanderson, the choir master, was standing at the back of the church and shouting for us to sing louder. I took a deep breath and projected my voice until it sounded strong and powerful.

As I started the chorus, I jerked in surprise, and my eyes opened when Jesse's soft tenor joined me. He was holding a microphone and staring down at me, and I realized that our voices sounded wonderful together. We continued to sing, my hands dancing over the keys as our gazes locked. My nervousness disappeared, and I forgot about the people in the bar as our voices soared together in perfect harmony.

My fingers played the last chord, and I rested my hands in my lap, still staring up at Jesse. There was a strange roaring in my ears, and as Jesse grinned and took my hand, pulling me to my feet, I realized it was the crowd. They were clapping loudly, stomping their feet and screaming their approval.

Jesse put his arm around my waist and kissed my cheek. "I told you," he whispered into my ear.

───

"I CAN'T BELIEVE HOW MUCH OF A RUSH THAT WAS!" I CROWED to Jesse as we entered the apartment. I kicked off my shoes and ran into the living room. I was still shaking, filled with a rush of euphoria that made my body buzz and my cheeks flush. I stood next to the piano and ran my fingers over the keys.

He laughed and stood next to me. "So, you're not mad at me?"

I shook my head and impulsively hugged him. "Not anymore."

He put his arms around my waist and pressed his body against mine. I leaned back and smiled happily at him. "That was a really lovely thing of you to do, Jesse. Thank you."

"You're lovely," Jesse said. He cupped the back of my neck and kissed me firmly on the mouth.

I moaned and, dear God, I wish I could say that I tried to protest, tried to stop him, but I didn't. I kissed him back immediately, sliding my tongue into his mouth and pressing my upper body against his. His tongue piercing rubbed against my tongue, and I shivered in pure delight when he cupped my breast with one strong hand and squeezed firmly.

"Jesse…" I moaned again as he trailed a path of hot, wet kisses down my throat. His lips found my throbbing pulse and pressed hard against it. When his hand left my breast and slipped under my skirt, I groaned and spread my thighs.

He broke the kiss, and I stared at him as he cupped my face, running his thumb over my lips. I opened my mouth, and he slid his thumb into its warm depth. I sucked hard on it, rubbing my tongue against the pad of his thumb as his nostrils flared and he groaned.

He pushed me down onto the piano bench. He swung my legs over it until I was straddling it and dragged me down to the edge of it. "Lie back, Del. I want to taste your pussy."

He pushed me back gently. I could feel the plush leather of the piano bench under my back as he pushed up my skirt and raked my panties down my legs. The air was cool against my throbbing pussy, and I cried out when Jesse buried his face between my legs. He nipped lightly at my pussy lips and then pushed on my thighs until I spread them as far as they would go.

"So pretty," he murmured and then his tongue was on my clit, and I was bucking wildly under him.

"Oh my God!" I cried out. He was repeatedly rubbing the little steel ball of his tongue piercing against my wet, swollen clit, and I was about three seconds from coming.

"Jesse! Oh God, Jesse!" I climaxed with a scream, my legs squeezing compulsively around his head and my fingers digging into his scalp.

I collapsed against the piano bench. My heart was thudding wildly in my chest as Jesse kneeled on the floor at the end of the bench and rubbed my shaking thighs. I stared up at the ceiling, panting as the rush of my orgasm faded and shame replaced it. What had I done?

"Del?" Jesse's hands were sliding under my skirt again, and I sat up and pushed him away.

"Jesse, I'm sorry, I… I shouldn't have done that." I stared at him in horror as tears started dripping down my cheeks.

"Del, listen to me -"

"No!" I pushed away from him and staggered up from the piano bench. My legs were wobbling, and I was crying so hard I could barely see him. He stood and held his hands out to me.

"Baby, don't cry. Listen -"

"Don't!" I stumbled down the hallway toward Cash's bedroom and slammed the doors shut, locking them behind me.

Jesse pounded on the doors. "Del, baby, let me in. Please."

"No! Go away!" I screamed. I sank onto the bed and curled up into a tiny ball, my body shaking with my sobs. I had ruined everything, just like I always did. I was a fucking idiot.

CHAPTER 10

"Little lamb?"

The click of the bedroom door was deafening. I took a deep breath and straightened my back. I had showered and changed into jeans and a t-shirt before packing my suitcase. My head was throbbing like a rotting tooth from crying, and I was dangerously close to vomiting. I stared out through the glass wall at the twinkling lights of the city and wiped away a stray tear as Cash shut the bedroom door and approached me.

"Hello, Cash."

He glanced at the packed suitcase at my feet. "Are you going somewhere?"

I couldn't look at him. "Yes, I'm moving out."

If he was surprised, I couldn't hear it in his voice. "Why?"

I wanted to lie – God, how I wanted to lie - but I sucked in another deep breath and turned to face him. "I broke rule number one." Another tear trickled down my cheek, and I wiped it away roughly.

"With who?"

"It doesn't matter."

I wasn't ratting out Jesse. I didn't want to hurt Cash any more than I already had, and if I told him it was Jesse... they were best friends and it would be awful for both of them. Besides, it was my fault. I wanted Jesse and Cash equally. It was a relief to admit that to myself finally. But fuck, I should have taken off before I actually acted on it.

"I want to know who it was." His voice was low and calm.

"I'm not telling you. Goodbye, Cash. I'm so sorry."

I said the last in a muttered little sob and hurriedly picked up my suitcase. Before I could take two steps, Cash had pulled it from my grasp and pinned me up against the glass wall.

"Little lamb, please don't cry." He nuzzled my neck. His soft words and the gentle touch of his lips against my throat made me cry harder.

"I'm so sorry, Cash," I sobbed brokenly.

"Shh. Don't cry." He wiped away my tears with his thumbs and kissed the tip of my red and swollen nose.

"Why are you being so nice to me?" I hiccupped.

He smiled. "Because I find it surprisingly admirable that you're refusing to tell me it was Jesse."

I gaped at him. "He told you?"

"Yes. Jesse isn't much for keeping secrets."

"It was my fault," I said immediately. "Please don't hate him."

"I don't hate him." Cash brushed a strand of hair back from my face.

"But you hate me," I whispered. My head throbbed again with a sudden burst of pain, and I swallowed back the bile that was rising in my throat. My mouth watered, and I pushed Cash away and rushed for the bathroom. I barely made it to the toilet before I was throwing up wretchedly.

Vaguely, I was aware of Cash kneeling beside me. He held back my hair and pressed a cool cloth to the back of my neck as I vomited until there was nothing left in my stomach. I wiped my mouth and leaned weakly against the wall as Cash flushed the toilet.

"Are you okay?" Cash crouched in front of me.

"I have a terrible headache," I said.

He turned away and rummaged through the medicine cabinet as I dragged myself to my feet. I stumbled toward the bathroom door, and Cash grabbed my arm. "Where are you going?"

"The bus station." I rubbed my aching forehead.

"Here, take these." He handed me Advil and a glass of water.

"Cash, what -"

"Take them, Del." He frowned at me, and I quickly downed the pills.

"Thanks. Take care of yourself, okay?" I smiled faintly at him and left the bathroom.

I cried out and clutched at my head when Cash picked me up and carried me to his bed. He stood me next to the bed and pulled my t-shirt over my head before unzipping my jeans and pushing them down my legs.

"What are you doing?" I squinted at him as he unhooked my bra and dropped it to the floor. He sat me on the bed and pulled my socks off before stripping off his own clothes and tucking me into the bed.

He joined me in bed and pulled me into his arms. "Go to sleep."

"I don't understand," I mumbled. "Why aren't you kicking me out?"

"I know you don't understand. I promise I'll explain it tomorrow when you're feeling better. Go to sleep now," Cash murmured into my hair.

I closed my eyes and wrapped myself around him like a

vine. I didn't know what was happening, but at this moment, I didn't care.

I WOKE UP TO THE SUN SHINING BRIGHTLY THROUGH THE GLASS wall. I squinted at the alarm clock. It was just after nine in the morning. I sighed and sat up, resting my arms on my knees and staring blankly out the glass. I had missed the bus, and there wouldn't be another one until tomorrow morning. I rubbed my head, thankful that my headache was gone. I slipped out of bed and used the bathroom before brushing my teeth. When I returned to the bedroom, Cash was sitting up in the bed. He patted the spot beside him, and I paused before climbing back into the bed.

"Do you feel better, little lamb?"

I nodded. "Yeah. I should get going."

Cash gripped my arm. "What time does the bus leave?"

"It doesn't matter. I need to go." I tried to slide out of the bed, and Cash tugged me against him.

I frowned up at him. "I don't understand what's going on."

"Jesse's my best friend."

My stomach rolled with guilt. "I know."

"Jesse told me a few weeks ago that he was attracted to you. I should have told you then. I know how – how persistent Jesse can be when he wants something. And he wanted you."

"I wanted him too," I confessed, blinking back hot tears.

He shrugged. "I know. I could see it when you looked at him."

"Oh my God, I'm such a whore," I moaned.

He frowned and shook me a little. "No, you're absolutely not. Don't ever let me hear you say that again, Del. Do you understand?"

When I didn't reply, he shook me lightly once more. "Do you?"

"Yes," I whispered.

"Jesse and I have a… special relationship, and because of that, I'm not considering what happened between the two of you to be a rulebreaker."

"What do you mean?" I blinked at him in confusion.

He sighed. "It's hard to explain, and honestly, I'm not sure I'm ready to try to explain it to you. Will you trust me for now?"

I nodded. "Yes."

I leaned against him as his hard hand stroked my hair. "Are you okay, little lamb? Jesse was worried about you. He said you freaked out a little."

"Yeah, I'm okay. I'm not sure I can face Jesse again, though," I said.

He hugged me. "Jesse's gone."

I stared at him in horror, and he hugged me again.

"Not because of what happened. His family reunion was this weekend, remember? He was catching a flight at seven this morning and won't be back until Monday night. That'll give you a couple of days. When he gets back, the two of you can go for coffee and talk about what happened."

"I really am sorry, Cash," I said. "I didn't mean to hurt you."

"You haven't." He squeezed me. "I know you didn't mean for it to happen."

"I didn't. I swear it," I said.

He kissed my forehead, and I stared up at him. "Are you sure I haven't hurt you?"

He nodded. "Positive." He gave me a thoughtful look that was tinged with dark lust. "Of course, that doesn't mean you shouldn't be punished for letting Jesse eat your pussy."

My pelvis was suddenly throbbing, and I swallowed thickly. "How do you -"

He smiled. "I told you, Jesse isn't much for keeping secrets."

He put one large hand on my bare breast and squeezed. "Jesse told me exactly what happened. He said you have the sweetest pussy he's ever tasted."

He tweaked my nipple, and I moaned as he leaned down. "He's right, you know. Your pussy is very sweet. I could eat it for hours. Do you want me to eat your pussy, Del?"

"Yes," I whispered.

He shook his head. "You need to be punished first, remember?"

I bit my lip, and he rubbed his thumb across my mouth before his hard hands closed around my wrists. "I think a spanking will help remind you that only I'm allowed to eat your sweet cunt. Don't you?"

I stared down at the bed. I was afraid that if I looked at him, he would see exactly how much the thought of being spanked again turned me on.

He put his hand under my chin and lifted until I was staring into his dark eyes. He smiled, and I flushed with embarrassment.

"Yes, I think a spanking will do quite nicely," he said quietly.

He pushed the covers back and sprawled me over his lap with one hard yank. He pressed down on my back with his large hand. "Don't move, little lamb."

He caressed my ass through my panties, squeezing and pinching while I squirmed against his hard thighs. I could feel his erection poking into my stomach, but he pushed my hand away when I reached under my body to stroke it.

"Hands out, flat against the bed," he demanded.

I obeyed him and lifted my hips when he pulled my

panties down to my thighs. His finger dipped between my ass cheeks and probed at my anus. I moaned quietly.

"First, I'm going to spank your ass and then I'm going to fuck it," he promised.

"Cash, please -"

Without warning, his hard hand slapped my ass. I jerked and cried out. It stung like fire, and I panted harshly but didn't resist when he spanked me twice more in quick succession.

"Such a brave little lamb," he said and rubbed my throbbing ass. His hand dipped between my legs, and he grunted in satisfaction at how wet my pussy was.

"Do you like being spanked?" His hard hand gripped my hair, and he tugged lightly until I turned to look at him. "Do you?"

"Yes," I moaned.

"Good." His hand smacked my red ass once more, and I cried out.

"Just one more." He raised his hand and spanked me a final time. I bucked against him as pleasure and pain soared through my body.

"Get on your hands and knees and spread your legs," he instructed as he pulled off my panties before lifting me off his lap.

I did what he asked as he brought out the lube from the bedside drawer. I twitched when the cold liquid dripped between my ass cheeks. He made a soft soothing noise as he rubbed it into the tight ring of muscle between my cheeks. When the liquid was warm and he could slide his finger easily into my ass, he coated his thick cock with the liquid and knelt between my legs.

He pushed gently between my shoulder blades, and I lowered my upper body onto the bed. My ass was high in the air, and he rubbed it again for a few minutes before resting his cock against my ass. He pushed slowly and steadily, and I gasped and moaned as he pushed the head of his cock past the ring of muscle.

After a few minutes, his cock was embedded deeply in my ass. He reached between my legs and rubbed my clit until it was stiff and swollen, and I was squirming beneath him. He hadn't fucked me in the ass since the first night he had taken me to his bed. In this position, I felt completely helpless. Instead of being afraid, I was almost embarrassed to realize how excited and turned on I was.

"Your ass is so fucking amazing," he said.

"Cash -"

He slapped me sharply on the ass, and I cried out. My ass clenched around his cock, and he groaned and twitched against me.

"Jesus Christ, Del," he muttered. "You just about made me come right there."

His large hands gripped my hips, and he thrust in and out of my ass. I was shocked all over again by the pleasure it gave me, and I moaned and shuddered beneath him.

"Touch your clit," he demanded.

I reached between my legs and ran trembling fingers over my throbbing clit. I tried to go slowly, but within seconds, I was rubbing firmly and dangerously close to coming.

"Del," Cash gritted out. "Stop."

I moaned with disappointment but did what he asked.

"Good girl." He caressed my ass, squeezing the cheeks before tugging my upper body up until I was resting on my hands. He rubbed the small of my back and then leaned over me and cupped my breasts. He squeezed them, pulling on the nipples before rubbing his scruff across the smooth skin of my back.

"Your skin is so soft," he whispered before licking the back of my shoulder.

"Please, Cash," I moaned. My arms were shaking, and I was desperate to rub my clit again. My right hand slid between my thighs again and rested against my clit.

"Do you want to come?" he said.

"Yes! I need to!"

He pushed my hand out from between my thighs, and my moan of dismay turned into a moan of pure pleasure when he cupped my pussy in his hand. He plunged in and out of my ass, one hand gripping my hip and the other rubbing my dripping wet pussy.

"Cash, please! May I?" I begged.

"Yes." He tugged on my clit, and I came apart around him. I screamed out my pleasure as he pushed into my ass and, with a hoarse shout, climaxed deep within me.

CHAPTER 11

"I'm sorry, Del," Jesse said.

It was Monday afternoon and we were sitting at the kitchen table. Cash was at work, and I had been hiding out in his bedroom under the pretense of getting ready for work. I had finally gathered my courage and joined Jesse in the kitchen.

"I'm sorry too." I stared at the table.

He reached out and squeezed my hand lightly. "Del?"

"Yeah?" I refused to look up.

"Just so you know – I'm not sorry for what happened between us. I've wanted you for a really long time. Hell, I wanted you even before you got together with Cash. I'm just sorry that I've upset you so badly. I should have known that it would upset you, but I was stupid and selfish."

When I didn't reply, he squeezed my hand again. "Are you okay?"

"Well, let's see – I cheated on a man who has been nothing but kind to me, with his best friend. I'm a cheating whore, and the worst part is that Cash doesn't even hate me for it. I don't know why he doesn't, but he doesn't."

Tears were sliding down my cheeks, and Jesse made a soft noise of distress. "You're not a cheating whore, Del."

I laughed bitterly. "We both know that isn't true."

"Please look at me," he said.

I tugged my hand free, wiped the tears away, and made myself look at him. He was giving me a look of guilt mixed with compassion, and I sniffed miserably as he handed me a tissue.

"This is entirely my fault, Del. You're not to blame for any of it."

I sighed harshly. "Stop it, Jesse. I'm an adult and I take responsibility for my own actions."

"You wouldn't have gone anywhere near me if I hadn't made the first move," he said.

I shrugged. "You don't know that. I've wanted you for weeks. Who's to say that sooner or later I wouldn't have made the first move?"

"Del," Jesse gave me an encouraging smile, "I promise I won't do anything like this ever again. Cash isn't angry with either of us. We can forget this happened, okay?"

I told him the answer he wanted to hear. "Yeah, we can forget it happened. Thanks, Jesse."

He frowned when I stood up. "Are you leaving for work already? You don't start for another couple of hours."

I nodded. "Yeah. It takes a while on the bus."

"You don't have to take the bus. Let me give you a ride. Cash's car is -"

"That's all right," I said. "I need some time alone, okay?"

He gave me a searching look and then nodded. "Yes."

"I'll see you tomorrow, Jesse."

THE APARTMENT WAS SHROUDED IN DARKNESS WHEN I ARRIVED home. It was early. Work wasn't busy, and by ten o'clock the bar was nearly empty, and Mark sent me home. I sighed wearily and kicked off my shoes.

I spent the bus ride and my shift trying to come up with a solution to what I had done. The problem was that I knew exactly what I needed to do to fix this – I just didn't want to do it. I sighed again and stretched before walking barefoot down the hallway. Jesse's bedroom door was shut, and the light was off, but I could see the soft glow of the light from the half-open doors of Cash's bedroom.

I stopped and leaned against the wall for a moment. Tears were threatening, and I blinked them back fiercely. I had only myself to blame for this. I ruined any chance of staying with Cash. Despite what he and Jesse tried to tell me, I couldn't stay in the apartment any longer. God help me, I still wanted both Jesse and Cash. If I stayed with them, I would destroy their friendship.

On the bus ride home, I decided to tell Cash tonight that I would be leaving. Now, I could feel my resolve weakening. I would tell him in the morning. I would give myself one more night of pretending everything was fine, one more night of being held in Cash's arms and then I would walk away. It would have ended eventually, I reasoned. Cash told me himself he didn't do conventional relationships, and my own experience proved I sucked at them.

Don't forget you're a cheater now, too, a small voice whispered viciously in my head. I winced and shoved it away. As much as I sucked at relationships, I had never once cheated. Despite Cash's forgiveness, I couldn't stop beating myself up for what happened with Jesse. I was a terrible person and didn't deserve Cash's kindness.

I took a deep breath, wiped the traces of tears from my face and moved to the bedroom. I silently pushed open the doors and stepped into the room. My jaw dropped, and I stared in shock at Cash and Jesse. Jesse, naked except for a collar and leather cuffs, was on his knees in front of Cash with his hands chained neatly behind him. I watched wide-eyed as Cash pulled Jesse's head to his cock with a roughness he'd never displayed with me.

"Suck," he demanded.

Jesse opened his mouth and latched onto Cash's cock. He sucked hard, and Cash groaned loudly and thrust his hips into Jesse's face. My pelvis throbbed as I watched Cash's thick cock disappear between Jesse's lips. Jesse took a deep breath, opened his mouth wide and slid Cash's entire cock into his mouth.

"Holy hell…" I breathed.

Cash's head shot up, and he stared at me in surprise.

I returned his gaze, wide-eyed and trembling. After a moment, he smiled reassuringly at me. "Hello, little lamb."

"H-hi." I couldn't look away from his dark gaze.

"You're home early from work."

"It wasn't busy, so they sent me home," I whispered.

"Come here." He held his hand out to me, and I dropped my gaze to Jesse, still kneeling at Cash's feet. He was staring at me with his eyes full of lust and need, and my sex throbbed in response.

I watched as Cash yanked Jesse's hair hard and turned his head back toward him. "I didn't say to stop sucking."

Jesse opened his mouth obediently and sucked on Cash's cock again. Cash smiled and beckoned me over.

"Come here, Del."

My legs trembling weakly, I staggered toward him. Cash cupped my face as he used his other hand to stroke and caress Jesse's face.

"Is this what you meant by a special relationship?" I said.

He nodded gravely. "Yes, this is what I meant."

He pulled me closer, and I leaned into his warm strength. His arm slipped around me, and when I looked up at him, he dipped his head and kissed me. I opened my mouth and moaned at the feel of his warm tongue as I listened to the sounds of Jesse sucking Cash's cock.

He released my mouth, and I stared down at Jesse again. He was looking at me as he sucked, and I could feel the heat in his gaze.

"Del. Look at me."

Cash's voice demanded obedience, and I tore my gaze from Jesse's and stared up at him.

"Are you scared?"

I shook my head immediately. I might have been trembling in his arms, but it had nothing to do with fear. I was so turned on I could hardly think straight. My face flushed as I tried to figure out what to say.

Cash searched my face, and he must have seen it in my eyes because he smiled. "You like what you see. Don't you, little lamb?"

I nodded, my breath coming in shallow gasps as Cash smiled again. "Good. Kneel beside Jesse, my sweet Del."

I dropped slowly to my knees beside Jesse and stared up at Cash. He used one hand to stroke my hair and the other to stroke Jesse's. "Unclip his chain."

I reached behind Jesse and unlatched the chain with shaky fingers. Jesse continued to suck Cash's cock but took my hand in his, squeezing it reassuringly as Cash smiled at both of us.

"All of it," he suddenly demanded, and I watched as Jesse took the entirety of Cash's cock into his mouth. I stared in fascination as he deepthroated him, barely aware of Cash's hand threading through my hair as he groaned and rocked his pelvis into Jesse's mouth.

He tugged on Jesse's hair, signalling him to stop, and Jesse released his cock. He smiled at me. "Hi, Del."

"Hi, Jesse," I whispered.

"Kiss her," Cash said from above us.

Jesse leaned in and kissed me. His tongue pushed at my lips, and I opened them, my hand squeezing his as our tongues stroked each other's. I could taste Cash in his mouth, and I groaned at the familiar taste.

"Undress her."

Jesse unbuttoned my shirt and raked it down over my arms. He tossed it aside, unhooked my bra, and then removed it. He inhaled sharply at the first sight of my breasts, and I made my own soft moan when he eyed them hungrily.

He looked up at Cash. "Please. May I?"

Cash nodded, and Jesse cupped both my breasts. His long fingers rubbed delicately over my nipples, and I cried out when he dipped his head and wrapped his full lips around one nipple. I watched as he pulled and tugged on it. It lengthened and hardened under his skilled mouth, and he used his teeth to pull lightly on it. He switched to the other one, licking and sucking at it until it was as hard as the other.

"God, Del, your tits are amazing," he groaned before sucking hungrily at them again. I arched my back as Cash took my hand and put it on his cock. I squeezed and rubbed it as I watched Jesse suck at my tits.

"Jesse," Cash said.

Ignoring my soft cry of protest, Jesse stopped immediately and stared up at Cash.

"Finish undressing her."

"Yes, sir." Jesse reached for the button on my jeans, flicked it open, and then pulled down the zipper. He yanked my jeans down, bringing my panties with them until they pooled at my knees.

"Lie down, Del."

I obeyed, and he peeled my jeans and panties down my legs, leaving me naked on the floor. He stared at the dark curls between my legs. His hands squeezed my thighs, and he looked at Cash again.

"Please?"

Cash shook his head. "No, not yet."

Both Jesse and I made soft groans of disappointment, and Cash smiled at us. "Both of you on your knees again."

We did what he asked, and he stroked our heads. "Little lamb, Jesse is going to teach you how to take all of my cock into your pretty mouth."

I swallowed a bit nervously but moved into position in front of Cash's cock. With his naked body pressed against mine, Jesse guided my mouth to Cash's cock. I opened, and Cash slid his cock into my mouth as Jesse moved his hand to my breast and played with my nipple. I moaned around Cash's cock, and Jesse squeezed my breast.

"The key is to relax, Del," he said, "and it sounds silly, but remember to breathe through your nose."

I nodded and, with my hands clenched around Cash's hips, took a deep breath through my nose and moved forward. Cash's hand petted me, and Jesse continued to pull and pinch my nipple, his breath hot in my ear.

"Good. Keep going," he said encouragingly. Cash's cock hit the back of my throat, and I started to pull back, but Jesse put his hand on the back of my head and stopped me.

"Breathe through your nose and relax your throat," he repeated. I took another deep breath and tried to relax as Cash's thick cock filled my mouth.

"Help her relax," Cash said.

Jesse nodded and disappeared behind me.

My mouth still full of Cash's cock, I looked up at him as

he ran his fingers across my forehead. "Spread your legs, Del."

I wiggled them apart. Immediately, I could feel Jesse squirming between them, and I released Cash's cock and looked down in surprise. Jesse was lying on his back with his head nestled between my legs. He gripped my thighs with his strong fingers and tugged my hot, aching pussy down to his mouth. His tongue slipped across my wet lips, and I cried out, my hands digging into Cash's hips.

Jesse pushed the lips of my pussy apart with his fingers and tongued my clit, licking it with soft, gentle strokes using just the tip of his tongue.

"Oh my God!" I cried.

Cash took my head and lifted it toward his cock. "Don't forget your job, little lamb. Take that gorgeous mouth of yours and put it around my cock."

I obliged eagerly, sucking hard on his cock as Jesse licked and flicked my clit with his tongue. I tried to relax my throat and breathe through my nose as I took more and more of Cash's cock into my mouth.

Cash was groaning and thrusting his hips back and forth, his hands holding my head steady as I squirmed and writhed on Jesse's tongue. My cheeks bulged as I took in more of Cash's cock with every thrust of his hips, but I barely noticed. I was breathing harshly through my nose, my lower body on fire as Jesse sucked my clit firmly with his full lips.

I moaned loudly, my lips vibrating around Cash's cock, and he groaned and shoved his cock deep into my mouth. My eyes were watering, and I choked a little bit. Jesse rubbed the steel ball of his tongue piercing against my clit, and I cried out with pleasure around Cash's cock. At my cry, Cash pushed further, and his cock slid down my throat until my lips touched his pubic hair.

Moaning and panting harshly, he pushed his pelvis back

and forth. My hands squeezed his hips, and I stared up at him. His cock was swelling in my mouth, and I cupped his balls gently, feeling them tighten in my hands.

"Jesse," he said hoarsely, "make her come."

Jesse's hands tightened around my thighs, and then he was sucking on my clit again, his tongue piercing rubbing roughly against the wet and swollen bundle of nerves. I screamed with pleasure. The sound was muffled around Cash's thick cock, and I came violently on top of Jesse's face as Cash rasped my name and came in my mouth.

I swallowed his warm seed eagerly, sucking and milking his cock dry as my body shuddered and shook, and Cash's hands tightened in my hair. He staggered back as Jesse slid out from between my legs. I licked my lips, smiling dazedly at Cash.

"Cash, please," Jesse pleaded. He was kneeling behind me. His cock, nestled in a thick patch of blond pubic hair, stood out straight and proud. The head of his cock was red and leaking a steady stream of precum.

I licked my lips again, and Jesse moaned. "Cash..."

Without asking me, Cash nodded. "Fuck her."

I squealed with surprise when Jesse pushed me roughly onto my back on the floor of the bedroom. He grabbed my thighs and yanked them apart as Cash sat down in one of the armchairs. After seeing him on his knees and listening to him obey Cash without question, his sudden aggression took me by surprise.

He knelt between my legs and shoved his hard cock deep inside my pussy. I cried out with pleasure and squeezed my thighs around his narrow hips as he plunged back and forth.

"Christ, she's so fucking tight," Jesse groaned. He stared at Cash, who was watching us from the armchair. "How the fuck do you even get your cock into her?"

Cash smiled but said nothing. I reached up and grabbed

Jesse's collar, curling my fingers into it and yanking his head to mine so that I could kiss him. We kissed deeply as he continued to thrust in and out of my soaking wet pussy. I traced my fingers over his chest as he licked and nipped at my throat. I found his nipple rings and pulled lightly on them. He ripped his mouth from mine and shuddered all over.

I pinched his nipple and then tugged on the ring again, and he swore loudly. "Fuck, Del. Stop doing that. You're going to make me come."

I grinned and tugged again. He groaned and grabbed my hands. He pinned them above my head, stretching my body out as he shoved my legs further apart and pounded into my pussy.

"Oh, oh, oh…" I moaned.

The teasing was done. Jesse was fucking me so hard he was bouncing me off the floor, and I braced my feet and thrust my hips back at him. My orgasm was starting, a tight pleasure building deep in my stomach and shooting down into my pelvis. I turned my head, searching for Cash. He was staring at us with a small smile on his face as he watched Jesse fuck me senseless.

I continued to stare at Cash as my orgasm roared through me, and he held my gaze steadily. My pussy clamped down around Jesse's cock, and he shouted and rammed into me one final time before I felt his hot seed soak my insides. He collapsed on top of me and kissed me on the mouth before rolling to my side. I lay there in a daze, panting harshly, and my body starting to tremble as the cool air swept over my sweaty body.

I opened my eyes when I felt strong arms around me. Cash was lifting me, and he gave me a soft kiss. "Come, little lamb. You need sleep."

He carried me to the bed and slid me to the middle of it

before climbing in beside me. I was sleepy and my body was weak from the orgasms. I didn't protest when he turned me until my back was against his chest. Jesse was climbing in with us, and I sighed happily when he pushed up against me. I was sandwiched between them, surrounded by hard muscles and rough skin, and I made a soft little moan of pleasure when Cash kissed me on the mouth.

I blinked sleepily and watched as Cash and Jesse kissed over me before resting their heads on the pillow beside mine. Jesse kissed me and palmed one breast as Cash put his hand between my legs and cupped my pussy, holding me tightly in place against his hard body.

"Good night, little lamb," he whispered into my hair.

I arched my back helplessly when Jesse plucked at my still-hard nipple.

"Jesse," Cash said.

"Sorry." I could hear the grin in Jesse's voice as he pinched my nipple, and my ass pushed into Cash's crotch in response.

Cash slid two thick fingers deep into my pussy, and I made a sleepy little moan as he moved them back and forth.

"She needs to sleep," Cash said.

"Just once more," Jesse replied as he pulled on my nipple again. "I love watching her come."

Cash must have agreed because his thumb rubbed my sensitive clit as his fingers thrust in and out of me. I cried out, my hands clutching the bed covers as Jesse slid down and sucked on my nipples as he cupped and caressed my pale breasts. Cash kissed and sucked my neck and the top of my shoulder as his thumb circled and rubbed my clit. The combination of their warm mouths and hard hands brought me quickly to my orgasm. My entire body arched as Jesse bit lightly on my nipple and Cash bit my shoulder.

I collapsed against Cash, my body as limp as a noodle.

Jesse released my nipple with a soft pop and slid back up the bed until he was pressed firmly against me.

"I could watch you come all night, Del," he said.

"Please, I can't come again," I said weakly.

Cash rumbled laughter behind me. "No more tonight, little lamb. Go to sleep now."

"Yes, sleep now," I agreed as Cash slid his arm around my waist. Jesse snuggled in closer, his breath warm on my neck and his hand cupping my breast. I felt safe and sheltered cocooned between their hard bodies, and I drifted into sleep.

CHAPTER 12

W hen I woke early the next morning, I was alone. I could smell coffee and bacon, and I slid out of the tangle of sheets, slipped into my shorts and t-shirt and padded down the hallway toward the kitchen.

My stomach was churning nervously, and I took a deep breath before peeking into the kitchen. Cash was sitting at the table, wearing just a pair of track pants as he scanned the iPad on the table in front of him. Jesse, wearing a faded pair of jean shorts, was standing at the stove and turning the bacon.

"Ouch!" He muttered when a sizzling spot of grease landed on his bare chest. "Christ, that hurts."

"Maybe you should consider wearing a shirt when you're cooking bacon," Cash said without looking up from the iPad.

"I know how much you like watching me cook in the near-nude." Jesse laughed.

"Yes, because bacon burns are sexy," Cash said dryly.

Neither of them had noticed me yet, and my stomach gave a funny little lurch as I watched them squabble like an old married couple. I guess I knew why Cash didn't fall in love with the women he brought home – he was already in love.

I cleared my throat, and Cash looked up. "Hello, little lamb."

"Hi." My smile was strained as I took a mug out of the cupboard and poured myself a cup of coffee.

"Good morning, Del."

"Hi Jesse."

"How did you sleep?" Cash smiled at me as I slid into the seat across from him and took a sip of the steaming liquid.

"Good, thanks." I stared down at the table as Cash gave me a searching look.

There was an awkward silence before Jesse cleared his throat. "What kind of omelet do you want this morning, Del?"

"Just coffee for me. Thanks, Jesse."

"You need to eat, little lamb," Cash said.

I traced the shiny wood of the table. "I've gained eight pounds since I moved in. I could stand to eat a little less."

Cash's hand appeared in my vision, and he squeezed my restlessly moving hand. "Are you okay, Del?"

I nodded and made myself look at him. "I'm good."

"Are you sure?"

"Yes." I extracted my hand from his grip and wrapped it around my coffee mug. I stared at the dark liquid as Cash sighed and Jesse cleared his throat again.

"Killjoy is playing at The Blue Lizard Thursday night, Del. If you're not working, I was wondering if you'd come by and sing with me again. Everyone loved it at Bill's."

I shook my head immediately. "No, I'd better not. I'm not good enough to sing with your band, Jesse."

He frowned. "Yes, you are. The guys in the band thought you were great, and our voices sounded amazing together."

He smiled at Cash. "You should have heard her. She's a natural up there, and our voices blend like crazy."

"I'm sorry that I missed it," Cash said.

I stood up abruptly. "I'm going to go have a shower." I turned and fled the kitchen before either of them could respond.

I STARED AT MYSELF IN THE BATHROOM MIRROR. MY FACE WAS pale, and my mouth was trembling. I sighed and brushed my teeth quickly before turning on the shower. I stripped and stood under the hot spray, blinking back the tears.

I didn't know what was wrong with me. Last night was fantastic. I got my wish – both Cash and Jesse had touched me, kissed me and made me come repeatedly. But now, in the cold light of day, I wondered what was wrong with me. I'd had threesomes before. It was always two girls and one guy, but what difference did that make?

I sighed and washed my hair quickly. The difference was that I felt something for Cash that I had never felt before. I didn't know if it was love, but it was certainly an emotion I didn't understand. If it was love, then I was in deep shit. Cash was already in love with Jesse. I was sure of that. I'd never heard of a relationship involving three people ever working out long-term.

Besides, even if I was in love with Cash, I wasn't in love with Jesse. At least, I didn't think I was. Sure, I was attracted to Jesse, and I enjoyed spending time with him as much as I enjoyed Cash's company, but that didn't make it love. I sighed again and rinsed my hair. Was I in love with both of them? The fuck if I knew.

The shower door opened, and Cash joined me. I kept my

eyes closed as he put his arms around my waist and drew me back against his chest.

"Are you all right, little lamb?"

"Yeah. Maybe. I don't know," I said. "It's just – you know."

"I do know." He kissed the side of my neck, and I leaned against his solid warmth as the water sprayed down on us.

"I owe you an apology, Del."

"For what?"

"I broke rule number one."

I stared up at him in surprise. "You and Jesse haven't been…"

He shook his head. "Not since you moved in. But last night, Jesse was – well, he was upset over his conversation with you. He was worried that you might move out and that he had hurt you. I comforted him, and it turned into something else. I'm sorry."

"It's fine," I said.

He lathered the soap between his hands and washed my arms and upper chest. When his hands cupped my breasts and his soapy fingers pulled at my nipples, I couldn't stop my soft moan.

"I don't want you to think that what you walked in on last night was some kind of retaliation," he said.

"I don't," I said immediately.

"I meant it when I said that I wasn't upset about you and Jesse." His hands squeezed my breasts, and I ground my ass against his hard cock.

"I believe you," I said.

He leaned over me and we kissed, our tongues seeking each other's as he continued to massage my breasts.

"Cash, have you and Jesse ever…" I trailed off, not sure how to word it.

"Ever what, little lamb?" His hands soaped my abdomen and then my hips before wandering between my legs.

I parted them, and he washed and cleaned my soft skin as I arched my pelvis into his hand.

"Uh – tag teamed a girl before?"

He laughed, a rich, warm sound that made me blush.

"No, Del. We have never tag teamed a girl before."

"Why not?" I asked as he soaped and washed my ass.

"We've never been attracted to the same woman before," he said simply as he tugged me under the hot spray of water.

He rinsed me clean and then kissed me again, his hands reaching around me to cup my ass and pull me against his cock. I returned his kiss as I ran my fingers over his broad chest. I rubbed the coarse hair between my fingers and lifted my head so he could trail kisses down my neck.

"Cash?" I moaned.

"Yes, little lamb?"

"Please fuck me."

"My pleasure, Adelaide." He shut off the shower and we toweled dry before he led me toward the bed.

I lay down on my back and spread my thighs wide as Cash nestled his large body between them. I could feel his cock probing at my pussy, and I made a soft moan of need before arching my hips at him. He slid into me, and we both groaned as my pussy gripped him. Before he started moving, I touched his face with my hands.

"Cash?"

"Yes?" His jaw was tense from the effort not to move within me.

"Why did you let Jesse fuck me last night?" I guess this wasn't the best time to bring it up, not when Cash was balls-deep inside of me, but I needed to know.

"I like to watch," he said. "And there's something about seeing the two of you together that turns me on like I've never felt before."

He gave a short, hard thrust as if to prove his point. I

moaned, my legs widening automatically and my pelvis rising to meet his.

"Did it bother you that I allowed Jesse to fuck you without asking your permission?" He was moving in slow, rhythmic waves, and I could barely think past the pleasure that was radiating from my pussy.

"No!" I gasped.

He stopped, and I whined at him, my hands clutching his broad back helplessly.

"Are you sure?"

"Yes!" I pouted and squirmed under him. "Please keep moving, Cash."

He moved obligingly, and I moaned in pleasure.

"Do you know what it did to me to see you under Jesse? To watch you with your legs spread wide around him and your arms pinned down, knowing you were helpless to stop him from fucking you?"

A shudder went through me, and he inhaled sharply. "You like submitting to me. Don't you?"

I nodded. It was pointless to lie. Knowing that Cash would spank me without hesitating if I disobeyed him did delicious things to my insides, and my pussy responded accordingly. I coated Cash's cock with a fresh surge of wetness, and Cash growled under his breath.

"Every day I hope you'll disobey me," he admitted. "Spanking that amazing ass of yours makes me as hard as a fucking rock."

I cried out in pleasure, and he kissed me hard on the mouth. "If I could, I'd keep you naked and in your collar all the time. Your only job would be to please me, little lamb. Please me with your wet mouth and your hot little cunt and your tight fucking ass."

I moaned, and he pushed his fingers into my mouth. I

sucked on them as he stared down at me. "Would you like that, Del? Would you like to spend your days and your nights bringing me pleasure?"

I nodded eagerly. It was embarrassing to admit it, but the thought of doing nothing but letting Cash use my body was exhilarating.

"That's my good girl," he crooned into my ear.

He was thrusting hard within me now, and my nails raked down his back as he kissed me before tugging on my hair. "Open your eyes, Del."

I stared up at him obediently, and he smiled. "The only thing that would have made last night better is if you were both wearing your collars."

My pussy clenched around him in response, and he jerked against me. "Fuck, Del!"

"Please," I moaned pleadingly.

He swore again, and then he was fucking me fast and furiously, and each hard thrust was driving me higher and higher. I gasped his name and climaxed, my orgasm washing over me in a glorious rush of intense pleasure. He muttered something I didn't understand and plunged deeply into me. I felt his warmth coating my inner walls, and I clung to him as he shuddered and moaned above me.

"WHAT HAPPENS NOW?"

"What do you mean?"

I was lying in Cash's arms, my head on his chest, and my fingers tracing through the coarse hair that covered it.

"What do we do now? Do we all start fucking like bunnies?" I asked.

"Is that what you want?" Cash's voice rumbled above me.

"I don't know," I said.

His large hand stroked my back. "We can go back to the way things were before."

"Can we?" I lifted my head and stared at him.

He nodded. "If that's what you want, yes."

"What about Jesse?" I said.

"Jesse knows I don't do conventional relationships."

"What if he gets jealous?"

"He won't. Jesse isn't the jealous type."

I rested my chin on his chest. Jesse might not have been the jealous type, but I wasn't so sure about myself.

"How long have you and Jesse been together?"

"A few years." He rubbed my back.

I sighed. I didn't know exactly what I wanted, but I knew I didn't want Jesse left out in the cold. Neither he nor Cash seemed to want to admit it, but they loved each other. You'd have to be a fool not to see that.

"I don't want you to stop being with Jesse," I said.

He cupped my head and tilted my face toward his. He stared searchingly at me. "Is that the truth, little lamb? Or are you simply saying what you know I want to hear?"

"No, it's the truth."

"Do you want what happened last night to happen again?" he asked.

"I don't know. Can I have some time to think about it?"

"Of course." He suddenly hugged me. "The original agreement still stands, Del. You know that, right? You don't have to do anything you don't want to. If you don't want to be with either of us, you're still more than welcome to live here."

"Thanks," I said.

He hesitated. "You need to know that Jesse still wants you."

I didn't reply, and he stroked my back again. "Do you still want him?"

"I'm not sure."

Jesus, that was a goddamn lie – I still wanted him desperately - and I tried to resist when Cash tugged my face upward again.

"Look at me, little lamb," Cash demanded, and I raised my head obediently if not reluctantly.

He searched my face again without saying anything. After a moment, I tugged my head free and rested it against his chest again. I knew he saw the lie on my face, but he didn't call me on it.

"Would it bother you if I were with Jesse?" I asked.

"I suppose it would be hypocritical of me to say yes, but in the interest of being completely truthful – yes."

I tensed against him, and he immediately stroked my back. "Only if I didn't know, little lamb. If you're with Jesse, I'd like to know. All right?"

I nodded, and he smiled down at me. "Because I like to watch, remember? And possibly record it for future viewings."

His comment made me laugh, and the slight tension between us disappeared.

"If you don't tell me when you're with Jesse, I'll consider it a violation of the rules and," he reached down and squeezed my ass, "spank you. Deal?"

"Deal," I whispered hoarsely. My insides were melting with pleasure at the thought of being spanked by Cash. Jesus, I really was turning into some kind of sex freak.

"Why don't you take a few days to think about everything, okay?" Cash said. "I'll talk to Jesse, tell him to give you some space and then we'll talk about this again. It's a lot to take in, but I was serious when I said that we can go back to the way things were."

I shook my head. "I won't ask you to stay away from Jesse. That isn't fair to either of you."

"Thank you, little lamb. But we want you to be happy as well. We're both very…fond of you, and we don't want you to leave."

I cuddled closer to him. "Thanks, Cash."

CHAPTER 13

"I hate the new girl," I said.

"What? Why?" Dana gave me a startled look. "Nancy seems nice."

I shrugged and heaved my tray of beer onto my arm. "She's been taking a coffee break for fifteen minutes, and it's busier than hell in here."

Dana followed my gaze. Nancy was leaning against the wall and talking animatedly to Jesse. Killjoy was on a break, and somehow Nancy had managed to lure Jesse away from the groupies vying for his attention. I watched as she threw her head back and laughed at something Jesse said before she rested her hand on his arm.

Jesse glanced at her hand as she stepped closer. Her breasts were nearly brushing against his chest, and he made no move to back away. My stomach tightened with jealousy, and I snorted angrily. What the fuck gave me the right to be jealous? He didn't belong to me.

I glanced at Cash's usual table. He wasn't here tonight. He was stuck at another client dinner, and I wished desperately that he had just blown it off. Maybe I wouldn't be seething inside at the way Nancy was so blatantly hitting on Jesse if Cash were here and giving me that dark look of desire I had grown to crave.

"What's going on with you, Del?" Dana had to shout to be heard over the crowd. "You've been in a mood for the last week."

I smiled apologetically. She was right – I was in a mood. Mark's new nickname for me was 'Snappy Bitch' and I couldn't even get angry at him for it. I was taking my frustrations out on them.

You wouldn't be so goddamn frustrated if you just gave in to what you really wanted.

I tried to ignore the voice in my head as I carried the beers to my tables. Unfortunately, the voice was right. I was frustrated because I wouldn't let myself give in to what I wanted – Jesse. He was giving me space, and I barely even saw him around the apartment, but Cash's comment rang steadily in my head.

Jesse still wants you.

Fuck! I still wanted him too. I had fucked Cash senseless every night this week. While I suspected he knew the reason I was so horny, he didn't bring it up. He just pinned me down every night and gave me what I needed – a hard fucking that left me weak and momentarily sated.

What frustrated me was that it didn't seem to be enough. I wanted what Jesse had to offer, too, but I couldn't get past my belief that if I started fooling around with both of them, it would ruin their relationship. A relationship between three people never worked out, I had lectured myself repeatedly over the last few days. Eventually, someone's feelings would get hurt, someone would feel left out, and things would turn ugly.

I took the bills from the customer, my body on autopilot as I worried internally. It was already happening, if I was truthful. Only, I was the one feeling left out and like a third wheel. I came home early from work on Wednesday night and let myself quietly into the apartment. I suspected that Jesse and Cash would be together, and my suspicions were correct. I stood outside Cash's bedroom, listening as Jesse moaned and pleaded, listening as their bodies clapped together in a quickening rhythm before I crept silently to the living room. I waited for them to finish, my hands clasped together tightly to stop myself from rubbing my throbbing pussy and tamped down my almost undeniable urge to join them.

When I heard Jesse's bedroom door shut, I crept to Cash's bedroom. I had crawled naked into the bed, smelling Jesse's scent on the sheets and on Cash's naked, sleeping body and feeling nearly frantic with lust.

I waited in the dark as my entire body throbbed with need and I willed myself not to masturbate. When Cash woke a couple of hours later, I attacked him. I almost begged him to spank me, but not willing to admit my neediness for it, I instead made myself come quickly while riding him. To my disappointment, instead of punishing me for it, Cash had simply climaxed along with me.

Now, I sighed moodily and stalked back to the bar. Jesse and Nancy were still gabbing like best friends in the corner, and even when I felt Jesse's gaze on me, I ignored them. Being jealous was ridiculous, I repeated to myself. Absolutely ridiculous.

I PLAYED THE PIANO IN CASH'S LIVING ROOM WITH HEAVY, pounding strokes, letting the music wash over me. It was two in the morning. Jesse and I had just gotten home from the bar, and I wondered briefly if the people below Cash were getting pissed by my playing and would put in a complaint to him.

Let them, I thought childishly and continued to play. *What's he going to do? Spank me?*

My insides throbbed with pleasure, and I pounded the keys harder. I wished bitterly that Cash was home to take care of my need. Why the hell did his client dinners have to last so long anyway? Who in their right mind would stay out with their goddamn investor until –

Jesse's hand fell on my shoulder, and I shrieked breathlessly and nearly fell off the piano bench.

"What the fuck, Jesse!" I glared at him as he sat down beside me on the piano bench.

"You're going to break the piano, Del," he said.

"Whatever." I could feel the heat of his body against mine, and I squirmed on the seat. My panties were already wet, and I wished he'd put a goddamn shirt on.

I scowled at him, and he gave me a slightly impatient look. "What?"

"Have you thought about wearing a shirt every once in a while, Jesse?" I snapped. "You spend all night at the bar with barely any clothes on. I'd think you'd like to actually wear some at home."

He shrugged. "I'm more comfortable this way."

"Or maybe you're just an exhibitionist," I said.

He laughed. "Possibly. The ladies at the bar don't seem to mind."

"Yeah, I noticed." I scowled. "Does it bother you when they literally drool on you?"

He laughed even harder. "I've never been drooled on, Del."

"Bullshit," I said. "That goddamn Nancy was drooling on you tonight. I saw it with my own eyes."

He gave me a thoughtful look. "Were you jealous?"

"No!"

"It's not a good idea to lie to me."

"Why? What are you going to do?" I sounded like a cranky child.

"Do you think Cash is the only one who likes to spank in this household?" he said warningly.

My mouth dropped open and I stared wide-eyed at him. "You're submissive like me."

He shrugged. "I'm what they call a switch, actually. I'm submissive with Cash but dominant with others."

I processed this new information as Jesse stared at me. It certainly explained why he was so rough with me before. Why he had pinned me down and fucked me hard. A fresh wave of lust rolled through me, and I swallowed with difficulty.

Okay, fine, I liked the idea of Jesse being dominant. But that didn't mean I liked the thought of him spanking me, did it? I enjoyed being spanked by Cash because it was Cash doing it. It wasn't the act of spanking that turned me on. It was the person doing the spanking, wasn't it?

"Were you jealous, Del? Tell me the truth this time, or I will spank you."

"You wouldn't dare," I said.

He arched his eyebrow at me. "Would I not?"

I licked my lips. This was a whole new side of Jesse I was seeing. He was usually so laid-back and easy-going, and I was unprepared for the intense yearning it brought out in me.

"Were you jealous?"

I stared at him and lied to his face. "No, I wasn't."

There was a flare of desire in his eyes, and I felt an

answering call in my belly. His hand gripped my arm, and he yanked me face down over his lap. I was still wearing my work clothes, and he shoved my short skirt up around my waist as I squirmed and kicked.

He held me down with one hand on my lower back, and I squealed when he pulled my panties down to my knees and slapped me on my naked ass. I twisted helplessly on his lap as he spanked me repeatedly, my pussy on fire and dripping all over his jean-covered thigh.

He spanked me until my ass was bright red and I was moaning and gasping. He slid out from under me. He stood at the end of the piano bench and tugged the button open on his jeans before sliding them down off his narrow hips. There was a large wet mark on the leg of his jeans, and I flushed with embarrassment as his cock sprang free.

"Suck my cock, Del. Right now," he demanded.

I surged eagerly to my knees, crawling forward on the piano bench and sliding his cock deep into my mouth. He groaned and thrust his hips at me as his hands wound into my hair and held tight. I had been practicing my technique on Cash nearly every night, and I swallowed Jesse's entire cock with ease, feeling it slip down my throat as my lips pressed against his pubic hair.

"Fuck!" He pumped his hips back and forth and fucked my face with deep, hard thrusts before abruptly pulling out. My moan of protest turned to happiness when he reached under me and rubbed my soaking wet pussy.

"You're so wet, baby," he moaned. "You like being spanked, don't you?"

I nodded as he straightened and guided his cock back into my mouth. I sucked enthusiastically, and his hand tightened in my hair. "Good girl. Touch yourself, Del."

I rubbed my swollen clit as I squeezed my lips around his cock. He rewarded me by teasing my nipple, and I made a muffled groan of pleasure. I was so close to coming that I could barely hold back, and I pushed my hips eagerly against my hand as his cock swelled in my mouth.

"Keep sucking, honey. Keep sucking." He moaned repeatedly as he thrust rapidly back and forth. "I'm going to come in your mouth and you're going to swallow all of it like a good girl. Do you understand?"

I squeezed his hips in reply, and he pulled roughly on my hair. "If you spill even one drop, I'll spank you again."

His hotly worded threat made me explode, and I screamed around his cock as my orgasm rushed through me. He groaned and shoved his cock deep into my mouth as he came. I swallowed eagerly, milking his cock with my mouth and swallowing every warm drop like he told me to. He tasted utterly intoxicating, and I cried out with disappointment when he finally pulled free.

"Jesus Christ, Del." He was panting heavily, his sides heaving and his entire body trembling, as he stared down at me. "You're fucking amazing."

I WAS LYING AWAKE IN BED WHEN CASH ENTERED THE bedroom. It was nearly three in the morning, and I was wide awake and, despite or maybe because of what had happened with Jesse, horny as hell.

Cash sat down on the bed and loosened his tie. "Are you awake, little lamb?"

"Yes." I reached out and held his hand. "How was the dinner?"

"Boring and long. They wanted to go drinking afterwards." He squeezed my hand. "How was work tonight?"

"Fine. Boring and long."

He chuckled and reached out to stroke my hair. "What did you do after work?"

I hesitated. "Nothing. Played the piano for a bit and went to bed."

He sighed, and I swallowed nervously as he stood and crossed the room in the darkness. I heard him open the closet door, and I sat up, holding the sheet against my naked body as I fumbled for the bedside lamp. I clicked it on just as he returned to the bed and felt a spear of dark desire in my belly when I saw what was in his hand.

"Come here, little lamb."

Still holding the sheet around me, I slid across the bed.

"On your knees and drop the sheet."

I dropped the sheet and knelt. He glanced appreciatively at my naked tits before taking the collar and buckling it around my throat. He pulled on the metal loop until I was looking at him.

"Hold out your hands."

I obeyed him, and he wrapped the leather cuffs around my wrists before petting my long hair. "I told you what would happen if you lied to me, little lamb."

I bit my bottom lip as he smiled gently at me. "I told you that Jesse wasn't much for secrets."

"I'm sorry, Cash."

He shook his head. "No, you're not. You deliberately lied to me. Didn't you, Adelaide?"

I didn't reply, shame colouring my cheeks as he cupped my breast and pinched my hard nipple. "I think you want me to spank you."

He was right. Despite my earlier spanking from Jesse, I wanted Cash to spank me. Needed it in a way I didn't understand. Although Cash made it clear he was fine with me being with Jesse, I couldn't shake off the guilt about what had happened earlier. There was a part of me that thought I deserved to be punished.

Or hell, I don't know, maybe I just really liked being spanked.

Cash sat back on the bed. "Come here, Del."

I crawled forward and draped myself across his lap, positioning my ass so he had easy access to it and resting my hands flat on the bed. My entire body was shaking with excitement and need, and I couldn't stop my moan when his hand caressed my naked ass.

"Your ass is still red, little lamb," he murmured. "Is it sore?"

"A little," I whispered.

"Did you like it when Jesse spanked you?"

I didn't answer, suddenly ashamed of my intense desire for his lover. Cash made a soft sound of disapproval at my silence.

"Put your hands behind your back, Del." He was pulling the thin silver chain from his pocket, and I placed my hands at the small of my back as he attached the chain to both of my wrist cuffs. I pulled experimentally at them, a little thrill going through me. We hadn't used the cuffs or collar since the night at my parents' house, and I was already starting to leak my juices onto Cash's suit pants.

I stiffened when Cash called Jesse's name.

"Cash! What are you doing?" I struggled to get off his lap, and Cash gave me a painful slap to the ass. I squealed, and he placed a heavy hand on my lower back to hold me still.

Jesse stepped into the bedroom, and I groaned with embarrassment as his gaze raked over my naked and chained body lying on Cash's lap.

"I'm going to let Jesse watch as I spank your delectable ass, sweet Del," Cash growled.

My entire body shuddered on top of his, and he gathered

my hair into a ponytail and tugged my head up. "I think you like that idea."

I wanted to shake my head no and deny what he was saying, but I figured I had already lied enough for one night. He grinned at my silent acknowledgment and kissed me deeply on the mouth before pushing my head back to the bed.

"Her ass is still red," Cash said. I thought I heard a hint of disapproval in his voice.

I jumped when Jesse's hand stroked my ass. "She was a very bad girl."

"Did you put the lotion on afterward?" Cash asked. His hand joined Jesse's, and I moaned and arched my back.

"No."

"Jesse." Now there was definite disapproval.

"She wouldn't let me. She just jumped up and left," Jesse said.

It was true. After my earth-shattering orgasm, I kissed Jesse and fled to Cash's bedroom.

"Little lamb?"

I turned my head and stared at Cash.

"Is that true?"

"Yes," I said.

He frowned. "You must always let us take care of you afterward. Do you understand? No running away or living with the pain. Am I clear?"

"Yes, Cash."

"Good." He slid his hand between my thighs and stroked my clit. I purred like a damn kitten and arched my back again.

"Already soaking wet," Cash murmured approvingly. "Jesse, would you like to feel how wet she is?"

"Yes, sir," he said hoarsely.

"Spread your legs, little lamb. Let Jesse see and feel how wet you are."

I spread my legs awkwardly, and Jesse caught my right leg as it started to slide off Cash's lap. He massaged it gently as he reached between my legs and rubbed my clit. I moaned as Jesse grinned.

"She's definitely wet."

He leaned forward, and I craned my head to watch as he kissed Cash. Cash gripped Jesse's head and forced his mouth open wide. I whimpered and moaned as I watched their tongues slipping and sliding against each other while Jesse continued to fondle my clit.

"Cash, please," I whined, squirming under Jesse's touch.

He released Jesse's mouth and stared down at me. "Please what, Del?"

"Please spank me," I begged.

"Whatever you want, little lamb."

Jesse stepped back, and I squealed when Cash's hand landed on my ass. It burned like fire on my sore backside, and I tried to stop the tears as he spanked me again and again. After a moment, I realized he wasn't spanking me nearly as hard as he usually did. I had a moment of grateful-ness for his kindness before he slid his hand between my thighs and thrust two thick fingers deep into my aching cunt. I reared up, my hands pulling uselessly at their bonds. Only Jesse's hands prevented me from falling off Cash's lap.

"Careful, baby." He bent his head to mine and kissed me on the mouth, forcing his tongue between my lips as Cash finger fucked me.

I sucked on his tongue eagerly as my pelvis rose and fell with the rhythm of Cash's fingers. I moaned with disap-pointment when Cash stopped and motioned for Jesse to step back. He slid me off his lap and onto the bed before unclipping the chain that held my wrists together.

"On your hands and knees, Del."

I obeyed eagerly and didn't feel a lick of embarrassment when Cash and Jesse stood behind me and studied my bare ass.

"Spread your legs wider, Adelaide," Cash instructed, and I scrambled to do what he asked.

"Good girl. Now, press your upper half on the bed and rest your head on it."

I flattened my upper body to the bed, spreading my legs even further and arching my back as I presented myself to them like a cat in heat. Moisture was dripping down the inside of my thighs, and I couldn't stop my legs from shaking.

"She really does have the prettiest pussy I've ever seen," Cash said.

"Tastiest, too," Jesse said.

"Why don't you have a taste? It's been a while since you've eaten her pussy," Cash said.

Jesse kneeled on the bed behind me and placed his hands on my hips.

"Keep your legs open wide, little lamb," Cash said. "Let Jesse taste every part of your sweet cunt."

I moaned loudly when Jesse licked me from my throbbing opening to my swollen clit. I could feel his tongue stud rubbing against me, and I made a loud cry of pleasure.

"Don't come," Cash said immediately."

"Please, please! I have to!" I begged.

"No, you don't. Self-control, little lamb."

"Oh, oh, oh…" I repeated breathlessly as Jesse stiffened his tongue and slid it into my pussy. My hands were yanking and pulling at the sheets as I tried desperately not to come.

"Suck on her clit, Jesse," Cash said.

"No!" I cried. "Please, I won't be able to stop from coming."

"Do it, Jesse." Cash ignored me completely.

"Yes, sir." Jesse's voice was muffled, and I tried to squirm away from him in panic. I would come for sure if he sucked on my clit. As much as I loved the spanking, I didn't think my throbbing ass could handle a third round.

Jesse's hands clamped down on my thighs, and he pulled me back. He spread them ruthlessly and bit me lightly on my inner thigh. "Be a good girl."

"I am! Please!" I whimpered. "Please don't suck on my clit, please don't…"

The words died in my mouth as Jesse's lips wrapped around my swollen, throbbing clit and he sucked hard. I managed to keep it together for about three seconds until he rubbed his tongue stud across it.

I screamed so loudly I'm pretty sure the people below us would think I was being murdered, and clamped my thighs around Jesse's head. My orgasm rushed through me, powerful and unstoppable. I twitched and moaned and cried out as Jesse continued his relentless sucking.

I collapsed on the bed, and Jesse raised his head and grinned at Cash. "She seemed to like that."

Cash laughed. "I think you're right,"

Jesse stood, and Cash pulled him closer. I rolled onto my back and watched in a pleasure-induced daze as Cash gripped Jesse's cock and stroked him firmly. Jesse moaned, his ass clenching tightly as he thrust his hips into Cash's hand. Cash dipped his head and kissed him deeply.

"I like tasting her on your mouth."

He licked Jesse's lips before giving his cock a final squeeze. "Move around to her front."

"Yes, sir." Jesse moved to the other side of the bed as Cash stood in front of me.

"Back on your hands and knees, Del."

I groaned breathlessly. "Just give me a minute to catch my breath."

Cash shook his head. "Now, little lamb. You need to be fucked."

My pussy muscles clenched at his words, and a spasm of pleasure shot through my belly. I forgot my weariness and rolled to my hands and knees, once more spreading my legs eagerly for him.

"Good girl." He knelt behind me on the bed and stroked my sore ass.

"Listen to me carefully, Del. I'm going to fuck you now and you, "he grasped the collar around my neck and pulled my head up, "are going to suck Jesse's cock while I do. If I see his cock leave your mouth, I'll stop fucking you, and you won't get another orgasm. Do you understand?"

I nodded, and he pulled roughly on my collar. "Do you understand?"

"Yes, sir," I said.

"That's my good girl."

I turned my attention eagerly to Jesse's cock. He was kneeling in front of me, and he stroked my hair back from my face as I opened my mouth.

"So pretty," he said as I wrapped my lips around his cock. "You look so pretty with your mouth stuffed full of my cock, Del."

I sucked eagerly, sliding my tongue around the sensitive ridge as Jesse groaned and threaded his fingers into my hair.

Jesse's hands were in my hair, and Cash's hand was still holding my collar firmly. I was utterly helpless, and I loved every single goddamn moment of it. Cash guided his cock to my pussy and pushed in with a harsh grunt. His movement rocked me forward, and I took more of Jesse's cock in as Cash gave a long, low moan.

"Christ, she feels so fucking good," he muttered to Jesse.

"She does," Jesse panted in agreement.

As Cash began to fuck me roughly, Jesse groaned and held my head. Each of Cash's strokes pushed Jesse's cock further into my mouth.

"Christ, Cash. I'm not going to fucking last," Jesse moaned. He reached under me and cupped my breasts, pulling on my nipples until I gasped with pleasure.

Cash grunted in reply and slid one hand under me to cup my pussy. He parted my lips and rubbed roughly at my clit as he pounded into me. I cried out around Jesse's cock, my voice muffled as Cash pulled on my clit.

"Oh fuck!" He growled as my orgasm rushed through me and my pussy sucked his cock in a tight, wet grip.

"Del!" Cash shouted my name as he thrust deeply into me and climaxed. A few seconds later, Jesse made a low moan. For the second time that night, I was swallowing his warm seed as Cash came deep inside of my throbbing, pulsing pussy.

The three of us collapsed on the bed in a tangle of limbs. I was panting harshly, my hair stuck to my face and wrapped around my collar. I kept my eyes closed as both Cash and Jesse carefully brushed and unwound my hair. When I was free, Cash moved me under the sheets and rubbed soothing lotion onto my burning ass before curling up behind me. I waited sleepily for Jesse to join us. When he didn't, I cracked open one eye. He was walking toward the door, and I called his name huskily. He paused, and I patted the spot beside me. A faint grin crossed his face, and he hurried back to the bed and climbed in beside us.

He cupped my breast and kissed me lightly on the lips as Cash put his arm around my waist. "I'm sorry, little lamb."

"Why?" I kept my eyes closed as Jesse pressed gentle kisses across my face.

"We should have asked if you wanted both of us together.

It was wrong of me to invite Jesse in without your permission."

Cash's body was tense against mine, and I squeezed his hand. "I liked it."

"We liked it too." Cash relaxed, and I snuggled back into him as I wound my arm around Jesse and pulled him closer.

Once again, I felt warm and protected between their hard bodies. I burrowed my face into Jesse's broad neck. "Good night, boys."

CHAPTER 14

I woke to the feel of a wet mouth sucking on my nipples. I blinked sleepily at Jesse's blond head before tugging on his hair.

He smiled up at me. "Good morning, Del."

"Hi." My back arched as Jesse returned to sucking on my nipples. Cash wasn't in the bed, and I squeezed Jesse's shoulder.

"Where's Cash?"

"Shower." He pulled my thighs apart and moved between them.

"We should wait for him," I said breathlessly. Jesse was rubbing the head of his cock against my clit, and I moaned. "Wait, Jesse."

He shook his head. "No. I'm going to fuck your tight pussy and you're going to be a good little girl and let me."

"Jesse, I -"

He was quick, I had to give him that. My legs were lifted and hooked over his arms, and his cock was thrusting deep into my pussy before I could react. He shifted his arms forward, pushing my legs back and out until my knees were nearly by my head. I was pinned down and spread wide open for him, and he grinned at me.

"This might be my new favourite way to fuck you, Del," he said into my ear. "I love how helpless you are, how easily I can slide my cock into you. Knowing you can't stop me from fucking you makes me so goddamn hard."

He thrust his hips back and forth. Each stroke of his cock made my insides throb with pleasure, and I moaned. He leaned down, and I squirmed as my legs stretched even further. I was feeling the burn in them now, and I pushed at his chest. He ignored me and kissed me hard on the mouth as he braced himself on his knees between my outstretched legs and plunged in and out.

"Christ, Jesse. She's not made of rubber." Cash's low voice rumbled above us, and I watched as he knelt on the bed behind Jesse. He reached between us and tugged on Jesse's nipple ring before pinching my swollen nipple. We both gasped, and a small smile crossed his face.

"She likes it," Jesse said. "She likes knowing that we can fuck her whenever and however we want, and she can't do anything about it."

My pussy tightened involuntarily around him at his words, and he groaned. "Fuck, stop squeezing, Del."

He glanced behind him at Cash. "Whenever I talk like that, her pussy practically swallows my dick."

Cash grinned. "She is the sweetest little submissive I've ever had."

He shifted on the bed behind Jesse before reaching into the bedside drawer. He brought out the bottle of lube, and I watched as he poured liquid over Jesse's ass.

"Ready for a new experience, Jesse?" Cash asked.

Jesse stiffened when Cash slid two fingers into his ass. I could feel his cock pulsing inside of me, and I moved eagerly beneath him.

"Stop moving," he groaned.

I pouted at him, and he pressed a kiss against my mouth. "Don't move or I'm going to blow my load."

"Don't you dare," Cash said before slapping him on the ass. "Control, Jesse. Use it."

"Cash," Jesse moaned as Cash pressed his cock against his ass.

"Don't *you* move, Jesse, or I'll make you stop fucking Del."

"Don't move!" I shouted at Jesse.

Cash laughed. "You heard the lady, Jesse."

As Cash slid his cock into Jesse's ass, I stared fascinated at him. The cords were standing out in his neck, and his arms were shaking violently against my legs.

"Don't fall on me, Jesse," I advised sweetly before tugging on one nipple ring.

He glared at me and cursed. I knew the exact moment Cash was entirely in his ass because Jesse made another curse before muttering what sounded like a plea for mercy.

"How does it feel, Jesse?" Cash asked before stroking Jesse's back.

"So fucking good," Jesse gasped. "Please, sir,"

"Don't come," Cash ordered. He wrapped his large hand around Jesse's shoulder and held him steady as he thrust. "Del, rub your clit."

Each thrust of Cash's cock sent Jesse's cock sliding back and forth in my pussy. I moaned happily as Jesse gave me a desperate look. "Don't do it, Del. Please."

There was a loud smack, and Jesse jerked against me. It sent his cock deep inside me, and I squeezed around him again as Cash made his own harsh groan.

"Who's in charge, Jesse?"

"You are, sir," Jesse panted.

"Good boy," Cash said before slapping Jesse's ass again.

I squealed loudly as Cash's hand threaded through Jesse's

hair and he yanked his head back. He studied me over Jesse's shoulder. "Rub your clit until you come. Squeeze Jesse's dick with your tight little pussy."

I wiggled my hand between our bodies as Jesse gave me another desperate look of panic. "Please, Del."

"I'll be quick," I promised with a small grin. I lifted my head and pressed a kiss against his throat before pushing past his hard abs and cupping my pussy. It was a snug fit with the way Cash was pushing against Jesse, but I wiggled my fingers until I found my hard and swollen clit. I rubbed it lightly and moaned as a look of desperation crossed Jesse's face.

"Don't come when Del does," Cash said.

"Cash, I can't stop," Jesse panted as Cash thrust back and forth.

"Yes, you can," Cash replied.

"No, I fucking can't!" Jesse snapped before groaning. He involuntarily thrust back and forth, and I tugged on his nipple ring again as Cash delivered another hard slap to his ass. It made all three of us moan, and I rubbed furiously at my clit. I was so turned on I could hardly breathe, and I ignored Jesse's cries for mercy as I tugged and rubbed at my clit. I thrust my pelvis upward as Cash drove in and out of Jesse. Jesse was panting and moaning between us, his face bright red and his chest heaving for air. I rubbed again, taking in my own gasping lungfuls of air as I stared at Cash over Jesse's shoulder.

"Cash, I'm gonna come," I moaned.

"Yes," he muttered as he drove harder into Jesse. "Fuck, yes."

At his words, my climax crashed through me. I thrashed against Jesse, my hips rising and falling. Cash shouted, and his fingers dug into Jesse's shoulder as he climaxed. Jesse screamed so loudly it made my ears ring before his back arched and his hips thrust like a wild man against me. He shouted again, every cord in his neck standing out in stark relief as he came deep inside of me. His body shuddered between us as he bucked wildly. When Cash pulled out of him, Jesse collapsed against me with a hard thud.

"Jesse," I whimpered as I pushed futilely at his hard body, "can't breathe."

He didn't move, and I was starting to panic when Cash rolled Jesse to the bed beside me. I lowered my legs, wincing at the pain and rubbing my thighs as Cash relaxed on his side behind Jesse. Jesse was moaning, his eyes closed and his body still shuddering madly. A little alarmed, I turned to face him and stroked his warm chest as Cash rubbed his back and hip.

"Jesse? You okay?" I asked.

He didn't reply, and I stared at Cash. "Shit, I think we broke him."

Cash laughed so hard the bed shook, and Jesse cracked open one eye and stared at me. I gave him an encouraging smile, but he simply rolled onto his back and stared at the ceiling as he gasped for air.

"It's okay, honey," I said as I rubbed his chest. Cash leaned down and pressed a kiss against Jesse's mouth before reaching across him and squeezing my hip.

"He'll be fine, little lamb. He needs a few minutes."

We waited nearly ten minutes for Jesse to recover as we stroked and rubbed his naked body. I was just thinking about getting up and having a shower when Jesse opened his eyes.

"Hey, welcome back," I said before kissing his shoulder.

He studied me silently before staring at Cash. Cash grinned at him and pressed a kiss against his mouth. "You okay?"

"Better than okay," Jesse said hoarsely. "That was the best fucking orgasm of my life."

"Good," Cash said with another grin. "Why don't you

relax for a while longer. Del and I will have a shower and then we'll make breakfast for you for a change."

"Sure, okay." Jesse's eyes had already slipped shut again.

Cash climbed out of bed. "Come with me, little lamb."

I kissed Jesse and slid out of bed before taking Cash's hand and following him to the bathroom.

———

"Adelaide, why are you limping?"

I gave my mother a guilty look as I grabbed a plate and dried it briskly. Somehow, I didn't think that telling her I strained my thigh muscles while having sex with two men yesterday was the best idea.

"Oh, I strained my muscles working out."

My sister Angela snorted as she jiggled the baby on her hip. "Since when did you start working out?"

I glared at her as my mother frowned. "How can you afford a gym membership?"

"Cash has a gym in his building," I said defensively.

My mother and Angela exchanged looks as I grabbed another plate. "What?"

"So, you're still dating Mr. Cash then?" my mother said.

"Yes, why?"

Angela used her shirt sleeve to wipe away the drool on the baby's chin. "You've been here all day and haven't mentioned him once. Normally, we can't get you to shut up about your boyfriends."

I didn't reply. Angela had a point. I usually talked a lot about the men I dated, but this was different. It felt awkward and weird to talk about Cash. I suppose it was because we didn't have a normal relationship, and I knew it was on borrowed time. It wouldn't - hell, it couldn't - last and the less I talked about Cash with my family, the easier it would be when it ended.

I shrugged and continued to dry the supper dishes. I could hear my brothers and father in the family room, shouting at the TV as they watched football. My other sisters had taken the older kids upstairs to play, and I was more than ready to go home. As my mother gave Angela another discreet look, I wished desperately that I hadn't planned to stay the night.

"So, are you and Mr. Cash getting serious?" my mother asked.

"Cash, Mom. It's just Cash, okay?" I said.

"Are you?"

"Define serious."

My mother sighed. "Don't be glib, Adelaide. You're living with the man. Are you going to marry him?"

"Marry him?" I said. "Mom, we've only been dating for a few months."

"Yes, but you're living together. It's obviously a serious relationship," my mother said.

"There has been no wedding talk," I said. "Angela, how did it go with your interview at the fabric store?"

"Good," Angela said. "Does Cash want kids?"

"I haven't asked," I lied.

"How old is Mr. Cash?" Mom asked.

"Thirty-five."

"Well, if you two are going to get married and bless me with grandkids, you'll need to get a move on."

"There's more to life than just being married and popping out kids," I said.

"There's nothing more important than family, Adelaide," my mother chided. "To be a mother is the greatest gift a woman can receive."

"I disagree," I said.

My mother's eyes widened, and she stared cautiously at me. "What are you saying?"

"I'm saying that I'm not sure I want kids," I said.

My mother gasped and clutched at the rosary around her neck before muttering a low prayer.

"Del! Apologize to Mama," Angela said.

"For what? Being honest?" I said. "So, I don't want kids, what's the big deal?"

My mother started to cry, and guilt rolled through me. Angela glared at me and patted my mother's shoulder. "It's okay, Mama. Del didn't mean it. She's still young and unsure of what she wants. Right, Del?"

My mother stared pleadingly at me, and I shrugged. "Yeah, sure."

"Just promise me that you'll talk to Mr. Cash about whether he wants children," my mother said. "There's no point in getting serious with him if he doesn't want kids."

A wave of depression rolled through me as I stared at my mother's tear-stained face. I would never be good enough for them. No matter what I did or said, I would never truly have their approval unless I married a nice man and had a couple of kids.

Maybe it was because I was tired, or maybe it was my own uncertainty about my future, but I couldn't stop my hot tears. I turned around and stared blindly out the window as I tried to pretend that my parents' disappointment in me didn't matter.

"Adelaide, what's wrong?" My mother's hands were on my shoulders, and she turned me around and scanned my face. "Oh my little Addie, what's wrong?"

Her childhood nickname for me made me burst into loud sobs, and she gave me a bewildered look before pulling me into her embrace. She rubbed my back and hugged me as I cried.

"What's wrong, sweetheart?" My mother wiped away the tears on my face.

"Nothing," I said before hiccupping. "Just feeling emotional, I guess."

My mother wiped at my face again before squeezing my hands. "You know what would make you feel better, sweetheart?"

I shook my head as she smiled at me. "Going to Mass. Why don't you come to Mass tonight with your father and me? You'll feel much better if you do."

"No thanks," I said.

Her look of concern changed to disappointment. "How long has it been since your last confession?"

"I have nothing to confess," I said.

"You're living in sin with a man and you have nothing to confess?" my mother said.

My anger flared, and I pulled away from her. "If you disapprove of my life choices, just say so, Mom."

"I just want what's best for you, Adelaide. Living in sin with a man isn't a good life choice and -"

"I'm gonna go," I said.

"What? But you're spending the night," Mom said.

"I've changed my mind. Angela, can you give me a ride to the bus station?"

Angela frowned at me. "Stay the night like you promised Mama you would."

"I can't. Can you give me a ride?"

She shook her head, and another wave of sorrow went through me. "Fine, I'll walk."

"Adelaide, it's late and -"

"It was good to see you, Mom," I said. "Thanks for dinner. I love you. Tell Dad I love him, would you? I'll call you in a few days."

I walked out of the kitchen, grabbed my bag from the

hallway, threw on my coat, and left the house. It was cold out, and I took a deep cleansing breath before shoving my hands deep into my pockets and walking down the sidewalk.

WHEN THE ELEVATOR DOORS OPENED INTO CASH'S APARTMENT, I could hear Jesse and Cash in the living room. I dropped my bag on the floor and wandered into the room. They had pulled the love seat in front of the TV and were sitting hip-to-hip, playing a video game. The coffee table was littered with beer bottles and a pizza box.

"There! There! To the right!" Jesse shouted.

There was the sound of gunfire, and Jesse hooted with delight before fist-bumping Cash. "Nice one. Let's try – Del, what are you doing here?"

"I live here," I said grumpily as I dropped into the armchair.

Jesse paused the video game. "I mean, why aren't you at your parents' place? I thought you were staying the night."

"Changed my mind," I said.

"What happened?" Cash took a swig of beer.

"Nothing happened."

They stared at me, and I scowled. "Nothing happened."

"All right," Cash said. "Do you want to play?"

"It's a two-player game," I said.

"I can take a break," Cash said.

I shook my head and stared sullenly at the TV. Jesse glanced at Cash, who shrugged before turning back to the screen. The video game resumed. Feeling more and more like a third wheel, I watched for about five minutes before standing.

"Where are you going?" Cash asked without taking his eyes off the screen.

"I'm tired." I stomped out of the room, grabbed my bag and headed to the bedroom. I ran a bath, climbed in, and sank into the hot water, staring moodily at the ceiling as I tried not to cry. I could still hear the video game, and I sank down until my ears were submerged in the water.

It was stupid to be jealous. I didn't even like playing video games, and just because my plans had changed didn't mean Cash and Jesse needed to change their plans to include me. Besides, they had asked me what was wrong, and I told them nothing. They weren't goddamn mind readers.

Still, it didn't stop the tears from leaking down my face. With a disgusted sigh, I sat up and quickly bathed before climbing out of the tub. I would go to bed and try to forget that I was a disappointment to my parents and the third wheel to Cash and Jesse.

I slipped on a pair of panties and climbed into bed. I stiffened when the door opened and tried to breathe deeply and evenly as Cash stripped off his clothes and slid into the bed behind me.

"I know you're not sleeping, Del," he said as he pressed up against me and cupped my naked breast.

I pushed his hand away. "I don't want to have sex. I'm too sore from yesterday morning, so you might as well go back and play your game."

I tried to wiggle out of his grip, and he pulled me even closer.

"Let go of me!" I snapped.

"Tell me what's wrong," Cash said.

"There's nothing wrong," I said. "I just don't feel like being mauled tonight, okay?"

I winced inwardly – God, I was being such a bitch – but Cash simply rolled me over to face him and cupped my face.

"Tell me, little lamb," he said.

"There's nothing to tell. I'm fine. I'm just tired and I – I…"

To my horror, I suddenly burst into loud sobs. Cash pulled me against him, and I buried my face in his warm chest and cried. After about five minutes, my crying slowed down to hiccups, and I took the tissues Cash pressed into my hand. I blew my nose and wiped my face as Cash stroked my hair.

"I'm sorry." I stared at his chest. I was too embarrassed to look him in the eye, but Cash cupped my face again and made me lift my head.

"Did you fight with your parents?"

"No," I said. "But my mom was talking about me getting married again and having babies, and I sort of told her I didn't want kids."

"She didn't take it well, I assume," Cash said.

I wiped at the tears that were starting to slide down my cheeks again. "She didn't freak out or anything, but it's like she didn't even really hear me. She can't even begin to understand that I don't want them. It's like I'm speaking a foreign language, you know?"

Cash nodded, and I rested my head against his chest. "She was pressuring me to talk to you about whether you wanted kids or not, and if we were going to get married. She wanted me to go to Mass with her and confess."

"Confess what?" Cash asked.

"All of my sins. Mainly, that I'm living in sin with a man. Of course, she has no idea that at this point, that's hardly a blip on the sin scale for me. She'd lose her shit if she knew I was fucking both you and Jesse."

Cash laughed, and the vibration in his chest was oddly calming. I breathed in his familiar scent and said, "I don't know how much longer I can keep pretending to be something I'm not."

"Then stop pretending," Cash said.

"It's not that simple," I replied. "You're not Catholic – you don't understand the guilt."

"You're a grown woman who can live her life however she chooses to," Cash said. "Don't let your family guilt you into doing something you'll regret."

"It isn't just the guilt," I admitted. "It's the disappointment I see in their eyes every time they look at me. I'm a failure to them – hell, I'm a failure to me – and I don't know how to fix it."

Cash weaved his fingers in my hair and tugged until I was looking up at him. "You're not a failure, Del."

"I am," I said. "I'm a college dropout working at a shitty dive bar and having sex with a man in exchange for a place to live. If that doesn't scream loser, I don't know what does."

"You're not living here because of the sex, Adelaide. You pay rent and do your share of housework and cooking. I've told you that you don't have to fuck me to live here. Do you think I'm lying?"

I bit my bottom lip before shaking my head. "No, but can you honestly say that you would have offered me a place to stay if you hadn't been attracted to me?"

"Yes," he said. "I wasn't fucking Jesse when he moved in."

"You weren't?"

"No. His roommates at the time had neglected to pay their share of the rent, and he was being evicted. I knew him from the bar and offered to let him stay with me for a few weeks until he could find a new place. We got along well and he's a great cook, so we made it permanent."

"When did you start having sex?" I asked.

He shrugged. "I don't know – a couple months after he moved in, maybe."

"Had you slept with men before Jesse?"

Cash was usually so close-mouthed about personal stuff

that I was fascinated with every bit of information he divulged.

"Yes," he said.

"When did you realize you were attracted to both men and women?" I said.

"In my early twenties."

"Does your family know?"

"They do."

"It doesn't bother them?" I said.

He tensed against me. "It bothers them a great deal. They're fundamentalist Christians and have very strong beliefs about the sin of homosexuality. They publicly disowned me, labeled me a hopeless sinner, and had members of their church send me hate mail. I haven't spoken to them in over a decade, and that's not going to change anytime soon."

"Why did you tell them?" I whispered. "You like girls too, so you could have just…"

His smile was bitter. "Pretended to be something I'm not?"

"I'm sorry, Cash," I said. My heart ached for him, and I rubbed his chest as I stared up at him.

"It happened a long time ago," he said.

"Do you miss them?" I asked.

"Sometimes," he said. "It's faded over the years. I threw myself into work when they disowned me, and that helped."

I studied him carefully. "Is that why you aren't married and don't want kids? Because your parents treated you so terribly? You wouldn't be like them, Cash."

He kissed the tip of my nose. "It's more complicated than that, little lamb."

"Is it?" I said. "If you were rejected by the people who are supposed to love you no matter what, it would make sense that you would be afraid to let someone close."

He kissed my nose again. "I think that's enough armchair psychology for the night."

I blushed, and he rested his forehead against mine. "Why didn't you tell me that we hurt you yesterday morning?"

"You didn't hurt me," I said. "I just have some strained muscles, that's all. I need to work out more, maybe try some yoga."

I thought that would make him laugh, but he just stared solemnly at me. "I don't like that you're hurt."

"It's no big deal," I said. "I liked what we did yesterday a lot. Maybe not as much as Jesse, but it was still really good for me."

He gave me a searching look, and I rubbed his broad shoulders. "I'm being honest, Cash. I swear. Where is Jesse anyway?"

"He's in his room. He knew you were upset and thought it would be best to give you some alone time with me."

"Oh." More guilt flooded through me. I was acting like a selfish, spoiled brat, and that wasn't like me. I suspected that Jesse had been looking forward to having Cash to himself for the night. Not only had I ruined it by coming home, but he was stepping aside so Cash could comfort me.

Cash turned me onto my side and spooned me, resting his big hand on my hip and squeezing it lightly. "Go to sleep, Del."

"We can have sex," I said. "I'm sorry, I didn't mean to push you away earlier."

"I didn't come in here expecting sex." Cash pulled me even closer and nuzzled the back of my neck. "Get some rest, little lamb."

"Okay," I said.

I closed my eyes and tried to clear my mind. An hour later, Cash was sound asleep, and I was still wide awake and restless. I slipped out of Cash's embrace and the bed. I left the bedroom, padded down the hallway and opened Jesse's door without knocking. The light was off, but moonlight flooded through his window, and I could see that he was awake.

"Del? What's wrong?" He sat up in the bed.

I pulled back the covers and took his hand, tugging on it until he climbed out of bed. Without speaking, I led him back to Cash's bedroom and got into the middle of the bed. Jesse was standing at the side, and I opened my arms and gave him an encouraging look.

"Are you sure?" he whispered as Cash snored behind me.

I nodded, and Jesse joined us in bed. As Cash muttered something in his sleep and slipped his arm around my waist, I pulled Jesse forward until he was pressed against me. I kissed his neck and stroked his hair before placing my mouth at his ear.

"I'm sorry," I whispered.

"It's okay, baby," he said.

He buried his face in my throat and cupped my breast as Cash stirred behind me.

"Okay?" Cash mumbled sleepily.

"Yes," I whispered. "Go to sleep, Cash."

"Sure," he mumbled again before moving his arm so that it was draped across both Jesse and me. Cocooned between their warm, hard bodies, contentment flowed through me, and I closed my eyes and slept.

CHAPTER 15

"If I go with you, it'll just cause problems."

"I don't want to do this without you."

I cocked my head and wandered toward the kitchen. It was almost one in the morning, and I was just getting home from work. I was surprised when I heard Jesse's and Cash's voices drifting out from the kitchen. Cash wasn't a night owl, and on the nights he didn't have a gig, Jesse almost always went to bed early.

"I want to be there with you," I heard Cash say, "but you know they're already suspicious."

As I walked into the kitchen, Jesse dropped his head into his hands and yanked restlessly at his hair. His voice was muffled when he said, "Maybe I don't care if they know."

"You do," Cash said gently. He squeezed Jesse's shoulder. "It's okay that you do."

I sat down at the table with them as Jesse lifted his head. "They think you're my best friend. It won't be that weird if you're there with me."

"The best friend story is wearing thin," Cash said. "Your family isn't dumb."

Jesse stared blankly at me. "Hey, Del. When did you get home?"

"Just now. What's going on?" I asked.

"My uncle died," Jesse said, "and I need to go home for the funeral."

"Oh my God." I jumped up and hurried around the table, sitting next to Jesse and rubbing his back. "I'm so sorry, Jesse."

"Thanks." He studied Cash again. "I'm not going to go."

"You have to."

"He hated me," Jesse said.

Cash smiled at him. "He hated everyone in your family. Besides, you're going for your mom, not him. She needs you there, Jesse."

"I don't want to go without you," he repeated stubbornly. "*I* need *you* there."

"When is the funeral?" I asked.

"The day after tomorrow," Jesse said.

"You can't get out of work?" I asked Cash.

"It's more complicated than that, Del."

"What do you mean?"

He glanced at Jesse, who sighed. "My family doesn't know that I'm bi, Del."

"Oh," I said. "Well, as long as you and Cash don't make out in front of them, it should be fine."

"They're starting to get suspicious of my friendship with Cash. I haven't had a girlfriend since moving in with him, and they find it weird that two men our age are living together. My sister told my mom that I look at Cash funny."

I smiled a little, and so did Cash, but Jesse gave us a miserable look. "God, I'm such a coward."

"No, you're not," I said.

"I am," Jesse said. "Cash told his family."

"I did, and look how that worked out," Cash said. "Jesse, it doesn't bother me that you want to keep this from your family. You know that."

"It should," Jesse said miserably. "It makes me a cowardly douchebag."

He stared almost pleadingly at me. "My family wouldn't understand, Del. They're very conservative and I'm their only son. If my dad found out I liked fucking men and women, it would give him a heart attack. And my mom... I'm a mama's boy and I can't stand the thought of hurting her like that."

I kissed his cheek. "You don't have to explain, Jesse. I haven't told my family that I'm sleeping with two men, and I'm not planning on ever telling them."

He stared at Cash. "I want you there with me."

"We can't always get what we want," Cash said sympathetically.

"What if I went with you?" I offered a bit hesitantly. "I could pretend to be your girlfriend and take some of the suspicion off of Cash coming as well."

"You'd do that for me?" Jesse said.

"Of course, I would," I said. I had no idea how I would pay for the plane ticket, but maybe I could ask Cash for a small loan.

"What about work?" Jesse said.

"I don't work again until Thursday, so if you don't mind going home pretty quickly after the funeral, I won't even miss a shift," I said.

"I don't mind," Jesse said. "Are you sure, Del? It's one thing for me to lie and to ask Cash to lie, but now I'm dragging you into it as well."

I smiled at him and kissed his cheek again. "I'm sure, Jesse."

"It's settled then," Cash said. "I'll book your plane ticket for you, Del."

"Thanks, Cash. Just let me know how much I owe you and -"

"I'll pay for it," Cash said.

I gave him a grateful look, and he smiled at me before leaning forward and kissing Jesse on the mouth. "It'll be okay, Jesse."

"Your parents' house is nice," I said as Jesse parked the rental car in the driveway.

"Thanks," he said before shutting off the car. He stared at Cash in the rear-view mirror before squeezing my hand. "Everyone ready?"

"Yes," I said as Cash leaned forward. "Do I look conservative enough for your parents?"

Both Jesse and Cash studied my dress. I didn't have many clothes, and what I did have wasn't exactly conservative. I wore a lot of tight shirts and short skirts and knew my usual wardrobe wouldn't be appropriate. I brought a dress that I'd worn for my niece's baptism and a dark pantsuit that my mother bought me for Christmas.

"Not enough tits showing," Cash said solemnly.

"Or ass," Jesse said.

I gaped at them, and they gave me matching grins.

"Behave, both of you," I said. "I'm trying to make a good impression."

The front door opened, and a short, plump woman waved at us from the doorway.

"Ready?" Jesse said.

I nodded, and the three of us climbed out of the car and made our way up the driveway.

"Jesse, I'm so glad you're here," the woman said. She gave

him a tight hug as tears slipped down her cheeks. "It's good to see you, honey."

"Hi, Mom," Jesse said. "It's good to see you, too."

He stepped back, and she hugged Cash. "Hi, Cash."

Cash pressed a kiss against her cheek. "Hello, Doreen. I'm sorry for your loss."

"Thank you, dear," she said as she turned toward me. "Hello there."

"Mom, this is my girlfriend, Adelaide Ford," Jesse said. "Del, this is my mom, Doreen."

"It's nice to meet you." I held out my hand.

"Girlfriend?" Doreen said in a soft voice. "She's your girlfriend?"

I nodded and squeaked in surprise when she threw her arms around me and hugged me. "I'm so glad to meet you, Adelaide."

"Call me Del," I said as I returned her hug.

There was an awkward pause as she continued to hug me, and Jesse tugged on her arm. "Mom, let go of her."

"Oh, right, of course." Doreen let go but immediately took my hand. "Come in, Del. I want you to meet Jesse's father and his sisters. They're going to be so happy to meet his girlfriend."

As she led me into the house, I gave Jesse a covert thumbs-up, and he grinned at me before following us.

"So how long have you and Jesse been dating, Del?" Jesse's sister, Joanna, asked.

"A few months." I took the bowl of potatoes from her, added a spoonful to my plate, and then passed it to Jesse.

"Are you living together?" His oldest sister, Janice, asked.

"Yes," I said.

"You finally moved out of Cash's place. About damn time," Jesse's father said. "You're a little too old to be still doing the roommate thing, Jesse."

"Actually," I said before taking Jesse's hand and squeezing it, "the three of us are living at Cash's house."

"What? Why? Don't you want your privacy?" Jesse's father asked.

"Stan, don't pry," Doreen said. "Cash, have some more roast beef, dear."

"Jesse's twenty-eight years old, Doreen," Stan said. "He's too old to be living with a roommate. Del and Jesse should have their own place."

I smiled at him. "Jesse and I discussed it, but I don't make a lot of money working as a waitress, so Jesse would have had to shoulder most of the living costs. I didn't think that was very fair, so when Cash said it was fine if we lived with him, I took him up on the offer. Splitting the expenses three ways instead of two is much more manageable for me. It's really my fault that Jesse still lives with Cash. Honestly, it's been great of Cash to let me move in."

"I don't mind," Cash said. "Besides, I barely see either of you. Our work schedules don't exactly match up."

"See," Doreen said to Stan, "they hardly see each other."

"You two met at a bar that he plays at?" Joanna said.

"We did," I said. "Secretly, I've always had a little crush on Jesse, so when he asked me out, I was thrilled."

"Are you two serious?" Joanna said.

"Joanna," Jesse said. "Knock it off."

I squeezed his hand again and smiled at Joanna. "We are."

"Thank God," Stan muttered under his breath.

"Well, we're so happy to meet you, Del," Doreen said. "You have no idea how happy."

She glanced at Cash and then at Jesse's father. There was

an undeniable look of relief on Stan's face as he turned to Cash. "So, Cash, how's business?"

———

"You were brilliant tonight, Del," Jesse said in a low voice as we climbed into bed.

"Why, thank you," I said. "Maybe I should give up this waitressing thing and become an actor?"

He laughed as he shut off the bedside light, plunging the room into darkness. The three of us were staying with Jesse's parents, and his mother had put Jesse and me into the larger guest room and Cash in the small one down the hallway.

I rested awkwardly on my side of the bed. I had never deliberately slept in a bed with just Jesse before. Sure, Cash went to work early in the morning and left us both in bed together, but this didn't feel quite the same. Jesse reached out and hauled me close until I was pressed against his lean body.

"Thank you, Del," he murmured into my ear. "You have no idea how much easier you've made this for me."

"You're welcome," I said. I kissed his smooth cheek, and he cupped my face and kissed me on the mouth. When his tongue traced my lips, I parted them, and we kissed deeply. He cupped my breast and squeezed it.

"Jesse, wait," I whispered.

He stopped, and I took his hand. "This doesn't feel right without Cash."

"We've had sex without him before," he said.

"I know, but this is different. The only reason he's not here with us is because he's not allowed to be, and that makes it feel," I paused, "wrong. I know Cash isn't the jealous type, but it makes me feel guilty. Am I making sense?"

He sighed and flopped onto his back. "Yeah," he said. "It does."

"Are you sure?" I leaned over him and rubbed his chest.

"Yes. Honestly, I feel guilty too."

"Okay, good," I said with relief, and he laughed.

I poked him in the ribs. "You know what I meant."

He rolled over to face me and pulled me into his arms. "I do. Thanks again, Del. For everything."

"You're welcome. Good night, Jesse."

"Night, Del."

———

THE ELEVATOR DOORS SLID OPEN, AND I STOOD IN THE FOYER of the apartment and slipped out of my heels. I rubbed my aching calves and then made my way in the dark to Cash's bedroom. We had flown home earlier this evening, and I went straight to work. Jesse was meeting with his bandmates, and I knew Cash was planning to stop by his office for a few hours.

When I entered the bedroom, Cash was sleeping in the bed, and a trickle of disappointment went through me. I was hoping he would still be up and waiting for me when I got home. I'd spent most of the last three days with Jesse and his family while Cash kept his distance.

I missed Cash. Missed him enough that it made me a little nervous to tell you the truth.

You're falling in love with him, Del.

Shut up! I am not!

You are, and you know it.

I'm not! I can't! He's in love with Jesse, I argued inwardly as I made my way to the bathroom. I put my hair in a messy bun, brushed my teeth and turned on the shower before ducking under the spray of hot water.

So what? You're in love with Jesse, too.

I froze, halfway to reaching for the body wash. My heart was racing, and my entire body was trembling. Fuck, I was not in love with both of them. That was ridiculous.

Maybe, but it doesn't make it any less true.

I groaned quietly and quickly scrubbed my body clean. I wasn't in love with either of them. I was just really horny. I hadn't had sex in three days, and I was confusing feelings of lust with love. The only thing I had missed about Cash was the sex. I certainly didn't miss the way he called me 'little lamb', or his surprisingly cuddly side when we watched TV. I didn't miss his snoring or the little laugh lines around his eyes, and I didn't miss the comforting warmth of his big body against mine. Nope, all I missed was his big dick.

I finished showering and slid naked into the bed next to Cash. Certain he was asleep, I squealed when he immediately turned over and cupped my breast. He kissed me with an almost frantic need as he toyed with my nipple. I wound my fingers in his dark hair and returned his kiss until I was panting and moving my body restlessly.

"Hello, little lamb," he whispered against my mouth.

"Hi, Cash." I arched my back encouragingly as he cupped and kneaded my breasts.

"How was work?"

"Fine, busy. I made quite a bit in tips to – oh fuck!"

Cash had slipped his hand between my splayed thighs, and I moaned happily when he rubbed at my clit.

"So wet, little lamb," he said.

"I've missed you."

"I missed you, too," he said.

I reached for his cock, filling my hand with it and rubbing firmly as he moaned.

He pushed one thick finger into my core, and I abandoned his dick and clutched at his broad shoulders. "Cash, please."

"Please, what?"

"Please fuck me. I need you."

"Do you?"

"Yes," I whimpered. "Please don't tease."

He pulled his hand away, and I muttered a curse before pouting at him. He stroked my inner thigh and gave me a look I didn't quite understand.

"How many times did you and Jesse fuck?" he suddenly asked.

"What?" I wanted his hand back between my thighs and tugged at it, but he refused to move it.

"How many times did you and Jesse fuck without me?" he asked slowly and deliberately.

My haze of desire lifted a little, and I studied him. The look on his face and the tone of his voice almost made it seem like he was jealous.

He isn't, Del. Cash doesn't get jealous, remember?

"How many, Del?" He slapped my thigh lightly. "Tell me the truth or I'll spank you for lying."

"That's not a punishment," I said. I was still embarrassed by how much spanking turned me on, but it wasn't like it was a secret or anything. Both Cash and Jesse knew exactly what being spanked did to me. I couldn't have hidden it if I tried.

Instead of his usual grin at my cheekiness, a scowl crossed Cash's face. He leaned down and sucked on my lower lip before giving it a sharp nip. "Fine. If you don't tell me the truth, I'll bring you to the edge of your orgasm and leave you there for the rest of the night."

His finger slid into me again, and he rubbed at my clit with the ball of his thumb, making me moan. "You wouldn't."

"I will," he said calmly. "You know I will. Now tell me how often you fucked Jesse over the last two days."

"I didn't!" I gasped out. "I didn't fuck him."

His thumb slowed and then stopped. He ignored my mewl of need and studied my face. "You didn't fuck each other?"

"No."

"Why not?"

"It didn't feel right without you," I said. "Cash, please. I'm dying over here!"

He sat up and scrubbed his hand through his short hair. "What do you mean it didn't feel right?"

"Jesus, Cash," I said irritably. "What do you think I mean? Both Jesse and I agreed that we didn't want to fuck without you there, okay? Can *we* just fuck already, or do I need to take care of business myself?"

He studied me for a moment longer, and I was just about to say fuck it and rub my own goddamn pussy when he pushed my thighs wide and stretched out on his stomach between them.

"Finally," I said as he bent his dark head to my pussy. He licked the lips of my pussy, and I moaned before wrapping my fingers in his hair. I pulled tightly as he licked the wetness away and then sucked on my clit.

"Oh God," I moaned, "that feels so fucking good, Cash."

I closed my eyes and rubbed my pussy repeatedly against Cash's tongue. When a warm mouth closed around my nipple, I jerked wildly and opened my eyes. Jesse had joined us, and I ran my hand down his naked body.

"Jesse? I didn't hear you come in," I groaned.

"You were kind of distracted," he said with a slow grin. He sucked on my nipple as Cash sucked on my clit, and I could barely stop my loud shriek of pleasure. I reached for Jesse's cock, rubbing it hard as my hips arched against Cash's relentless tongue. With both of their hot mouths working me over, it didn't take long for my orgasm to wash over me. I writhed and twisted and moaned both of their names as Cash traced the lips of my pussy with his tongue before sitting up.

I watched as he and Jesse kissed before Cash stretched out on my right side. Jesse was on my left, and they each leaned down and sucked at my nipples. I cupped Cash's dark head in one hand and Jesse's blond head in the other as warmth and desire flooded through me. God, the two of them were perfection.

Cash raised his head and smiled at me. "You're perfect, sweet Del."

I stroked the dark stubble on his jaw. "I was just thinking the same thing about you and Jesse."

Jesse pressed a warm kiss on my throat as Cash rubbed my hip with his big hand.

"Cash?"

"Hmm?" He was kissing my collarbone, and I tugged on his hair until he lifted his head.

"I want both of you."

"You have us," he replied before kissing me.

"No, I mean, I want to fuck both of you. At the same time."

Jesse's hand, which had slipped between my legs, slowed to a stop, and he and Cash stared silently at each other. The three of us had been together for weeks now, but I'd never had sex with both men at once. Cash's cock was so big, and Jesse wasn't exactly small either, that I had balked at taking both of them. To my relief, they hadn't pushed me about it. It was irrational and stupid, but I was afraid that it would either hurt very badly or permanently wreck my lady parts. Now, suddenly, I wanted it. Wanted it so much I could barely think straight. It was dumb to believe either Cash or Jesse would hurt me.

"You said you didn't want that, little lamb," Cash said.

"I changed my mind," I said.

"Are you sure, baby?" Jesse asked. "You know we're okay with not doing that."

"I'm sure," I said. "But we need to go slow, and if I start hollering for you to stop, you have to promise me you will."

"We will," Cash said. His voice was calm, but I could see the excitement in his eyes as he glanced at Jesse again.

Jesse hesitated a moment before nodding. "We won't hurt you, Del. I promise."

"I know." I sat up and cracked my knuckles before rolling my shoulders like a boxer. "All right, I'm ready. Let's do this, boys."

They both laughed, and the slight tension between us disappeared.

"Do you have a preference for who goes where?" Cash asked.

"You in my pussy and Jesse in my ass," I said. Knowing how much Cash loved fucking my ass, I added, "This time. Assuming this goes well, and you guys don't wreck my lady parts, we can switch it up the next time. Okay?"

Jesse kissed the back of my shoulder. "I promise we will not wreck your lady parts."

He said it so solemnly that I giggled as Cash reached into the bedside drawer and took out the bottle of lube. He handed it to Jesse, and I straddled Cash's hips before leaning down and kissing him.

He returned my kiss, cupping my face tenderly before whispering, "Thank you, Del."

"Don't thank me yet. I might tap out before we actually do it," I said.

He smiled and cupped my breasts, pulling on my nipples as Jesse stroked my back with his warm hands. I turned my head, and Jesse and I kissed as Cash watched. When we broke apart, Cash was smiling at both of us, and I leaned down and kissed him again before rising to my knees. Cash guided his cock into my pussy, and I moaned happily as I sank onto his thick cock.

I rode him slowly as he played with my breasts and was only vaguely aware of Jesse moving behind me. Cash spread his legs wide, and Jesse nestled his body between them. He rubbed his cock against my ass, and I moaned in encouragement. He pressed his warm hand between my shoulder blades, and I bent over Cash, resting my hands on either side of his head. Cash cupped my face and kissed me again, swallowing my soft little gasp when Jesse poured lube over my ass. It was cold, but his hands warmed it up as he rubbed and stroked my ass. The feel of his finger sliding into my ass made me cry out, and I pushed back against him eagerly.

Cash rubbed his thumb across my bottom lip. "It's going to feel so good for you, little lamb."

"I hope so," I panted. Jesse had pushed a second finger into my ass, and already I was starting to feel a little anxious.

"Are you nervous?" Cash said.

I nodded, and he smoothed my hair back from my face. "Don't be. We'll stop if it's too much. Okay?"

"Okay," I said.

Behind me, Jesse was smoothing lube over his cock. When I felt the blunt head touch my ass, I tensed, and Cash made a soothing noise before squeezing my breasts. His rough fingers rubbing my nipples sent a new bolt of lust through me, and I arched my back as Jesse pushed experimentally.

He groaned loudly when the head of his cock pushed past my tight ring of muscle. I squeaked and arched my back again as Jesse said hoarsely, "Okay, baby?"

"Yes," I gasped. "I'm good."

I tightened around Cash's cock when Jesse pushed again, and Cash made his own harsh groan.

"Little lamb, don't squeeze like that or I'm going to blow my load before we even get started."

"I'm sorry," I moaned. "I can't help it."

Cash moved his hands to my waist. "Jesse, hurry," he said in a strangled voice.

"No, don't hurry," I said. I was fascinated by how Cash, who never seemed to lose control, was acting. His breath was coming in harsh, quick pants, and the look on his face suggested he was about to lose it completely.

"Cash, are *you* okay?" I said.

"Yes...no...fuck!" He gritted out as Jesse pushed again, and I squeezed involuntarily.

Jesse's hand slid around my body, and he cupped my breasts as he made one final push and filled my ass.

"Fuck!" I shouted. I felt stretched and full to the brim, and all three of us stayed perfectly still as I waited for my body to adjust.

After a couple of minutes, I carefully straightened and rested my shaking hands on Cash's broad chest. Jesse was warm and solid against my back, and I stared into Cash's dark eyes as he caressed my waist.

"Okay?" he gasped.

"Yes." I moved experimentally, a ripple of power rolling through me when both men groaned loudly.

"Oh Jesus," Jesse said. "This was not a good fucking idea. If I last longer than a minute, I'll be surprised."

I couldn't help my giggle, and they both groaned again at the movement of my body.

"Hold still," Cash groaned.

"It's not going to work if I don't move." I was utterly fascinated by their reaction, and I braced my hands, lifting my body up and down. Cash cried out, his hands tightening painfully on my waist as Jesse made two wild thrusts in my ass.

"Jesse!" Cash said. "Don't fucking do that."

"I can't help it," Jesse groaned. "She's so fucking tight, Cash. I can feel you and I can…"

He moaned helplessly when Cash made a slow thrust of his own.

"Oh God," I whispered. "So good…"

"Rub your clit," Cash ordered as his hands settled on my hips.

"I won't last long if I do," I warned.

"Fuck, and you think we will?" Jesse groaned. He pressed his lips against the side of my throat as he kneaded my breasts. "Touch your clit, baby."

I brushed the tips of my fingers against my clit and cried out at the sensation. Below me, Cash was moving his hips, and every stroke of his cock lit me on fire. Jesse pushed lightly on my back, and I leaned over Cash again, bracing my hand on his shoulder as the two men started a shaky rhythm of thrusting.

As Cash thrust in, Jesse withdrew, and I shook helplessly between them as intense pleasure radiated through my body. I rubbed my clit, crying out with every thrust. The hard stroking of Jesse's cock made me clench my pussy around Cash, and every time I tightened, he groaned loudly.

Hell, both men were panting and moaning, but I barely heard them. The only thing that mattered was the orgasm that was dancing just out of my reach. I chased it, rubbing my clit with hard and furious strokes as Jesse and Cash moved harder and faster. They were starting to lose their careful rhythm, but I barely noticed. Cash's hand knocked mine away from my pussy. At the feel of his rough fingers against my swollen, throbbing clit, I shrieked and climaxed immediately, my ass and pussy tightening around their hard cocks.

I shook wildly as Jesse stiffened behind me. His hands gripped my breasts, and he made a loud cry as he came deep in my ass. Cash thrust hard and fast before shouting and arching his hips a final time. Warm wetness flooded my pussy, and I ground my pelvis against his as he shuddered beneath me.

When Jesse pulled out and collapsed on the bed next to us, I dropped onto Cash. His heart was beating like a jackhammer beneath my ear, and he was shaking almost violently. I closed my eyes and tried to control my breathing as Cash wrapped his large arms around my waist and pressed kisses against my face.

"Did we hurt you, little lamb?" he murmured into my ear.

I shook my head and kissed his chest as Cash reached out and stroked Jesse's thigh. Jesse stared dazedly at him before his gaze fell to me.

"Del? Okay?" he said.

"Better than okay," I said.

Cash eased me off of him, and I lay between them as they rubbed and stroked my naked body with their warm hands.

"That was incredible, little lamb," Cash said. "Thank you."

I smiled at him. "I should be thanking you. I don't think I've ever come that hard in my life."

"You and me both," Jesse said. "Fuck, you really are perfect, Del."

We rested quietly, and both men were nearly asleep when I crawled over Cash and headed to the bathroom. When I returned, they were sleeping and spooning in the middle of the bed. I hesitated before climbing into the bed behind Cash. I pressed my body against his back and stroked his hip. He muttered in his sleep and moved closer to Jesse, holding him tightly as jealousy bloomed in my belly. I sighed and rested my forehead against his back, blinking back the hot tears.

Don't, Del, I told myself. *You just had the most incredible experience of your life. Don't ruin the moment with pettiness and jealousy.*

Solid advice, but it didn't help. I was jealous. I was in love with Cash and Jesse, and there was no point in denying it any longer. I was in love with them, and neither of them would ever love me the way they loved each other. How could they? They had been together for years, and I was just the girl they both lusted after.

You know it's more than that, Del.

Did I? Or was that just my heart hoping it was more? I honestly didn't know. Cash had warned me not to fall in love with him, and at the time, it had been so easy to say I wouldn't. I'd never been in love before, hadn't thought I was capable of it, to be truthful.

The tears spilled down my cheeks as I flipped to my back and stared at the ceiling. I knew nothing about being in love, but I didn't think it should be this painful. I tried to picture myself living with Cash and Jesse, being in love with both of them, and always feeling like the piece of the puzzle that didn't quite fit, no matter how hard you tried to push it into place.

My stomach rolled with nausea. I couldn't do this. I couldn't live with them - couldn't *love* them - knowing that they would never feel the same way about me. If I tried, my jealousy would eventually tear us all apart, and I wouldn't do that to them. They didn't deserve that.

I turned away from Cash and Jesse and wept quietly as they slept.

CHAPTER 16

My suitcase was packed when Cash came home from work the next night. I stood in the kitchen, waiting nervously for him as he hung up his jacket and took off his shoes. Jesse was at a gig, and although I felt guilty for doing this when he wasn't here, I wasn't strong enough to say goodbye to both of them at once.

Cash walked into the kitchen and jerked in surprise. I was supposed to be at work, and my heart clenched painfully in my chest when he gave me a warm smile. "Del? What are you doing home?"

I didn't reply. My carefully planned goodbye speech had flown out the window at the sight of Cash. He gave me a worried look, and I backed away when he reached for me.

"Little lamb? Why aren't you at work?"

"I quit my job today," I said. Mark was beyond pissed at me when I quit without any notice, but Killjoy was playing the bar tomorrow night. There was no way in hell I could continue to work there, knowing I'd see Jesse and Cash once a month.

"You quit your job?" He frowned and took another step

toward me. His foot hit my bag, and he stared at it for a moment before raising his gaze to mine. "What's going on?"

"I'm leaving," I said.

A look of dismay flickered across his face. "Is this about last night? We don't have to do that again, Del. If it wasn't what you wanted, both Jesse and I are perfectly fine with not -"

"It's not that," I said.

"Then what is it?"

"I broke rule number four." My voice broke, and I cleared my throat as Cash stared cautiously at me.

My stomach was in knots, and my heart was thudding like a drum as I waited and hoped for him to say he loved me. As the silence spun out between us, my body grew more and more tense until I blurted out, "I'm sorry."

"Del," he said. "I told you not to fall in love with me."

"I know." My heart broke at the look of confusion and sorrow on his face, and I grabbed my suitcase. "I left my keys on the hallway table. Will you tell Jesse I said goodbye?"

"Where are you going to go?"

"My parents' place for a bit. After that, I don't know. I'll figure it out." I stood on my tiptoes and pressed my lips against his cheek. "Goodbye, Cash. Thank you for everything."

I slipped past him with tears pricking at my eyes and my throat burning. When he called my name, my heart beat fiercely and I turned back. The hope building in my chest died when he said, "Take care of yourself, little lamb."

"You too, Cash." I fled the kitchen, running down the hall and hitting the button for the elevator. The doors opened, and I stepped inside and turned around, a part of me hoping to see Cash standing in the hallway. It was empty, and I sobbed bitterly as the doors closed and the elevator moved smoothly downward.

"ADELAIDE, YOU'VE BEEN MOPING FOR TOO LONG. YOU NEED to get out of the house," my mother said as she entered the living room. I was sitting in the window seat, staring at the falling snow, and my mother sat down next to me.

"Why don't you come to Mass with your father and me?"

"No, thank you."

"I know you're upset about your breakup with Mr. Cash, but you can't stay in the house forever. You need to do something."

"It's only been a week," I said. "Jesus, Mom, cut me some slack."

"Don't use that language in our house, please," my mother said. "You know the rules."

"I know. Sorry."

"Adelaide," my mother rested her hand on top of mine, "we're worried about you. You've never been so upset about breaking up with a boy before. Will you tell me what happened? Does Mr. Cash not want," she hesitated, "children?"

"Mom, please," I groaned, "I don't want to talk about it. Besides, it doesn't matter if he wants children or not. I don't want children, remember?"

"I know you keep saying that," my mother said, "but you're young and -"

"I'm old enough to know that I don't want kids," I said.

My mother stared at me in disappointment, but for once it didn't bring on even a lick of guilt. Being without Cash and Jesse for the last week had flipped some kind of switch in me. All I could think about was how much I missed them, and I didn't give a damn what my mother or anyone else in my life thought about me.

Call Cash, my inner voice whispered persuasively. *Call him and tell him you made a terrible mistake.*

I couldn't call him. He didn't love me, and I couldn't go back to the way things were. Fuck, who knew that being in love would be this goddamn painful?

The doorbell rang, and my mother patted my knee before standing. "Think about going to Mass, Adelaide. It will be good for you."

I didn't reply and continued to stare out the window as she left the room. The front door opened, and I shot to my feet when I heard Jesse's voice asking for me. I ran out of the living room and skidded into the hallway, staring numbly at Jesse as he smiled at my mother.

"Who are you?" she said.

"My name is Jesse. I'm a friend of Del's, and I wondered if I could speak with her for a moment."

"Jesse," I whispered. "What are you doing here?"

My mother turned and frowned when she saw my face. "Adelaide, what's wrong?"

"Nothing," I said. "Can you give us a minute?"

She hesitated before retreating to the kitchen. Jesse stood in the hallway with snow melting in his blond hair. It took everything in me not to throw myself into his arms.

"Hi, Del," he said.

"What are you doing here?" I said.

"I wanted to talk with you about Cash and -"

"Not here." I glanced at the kitchen. No doubt my mother was standing just inside the doorway, listening to everything.

"Go for a drive with me?" Jesse asked.

"That's not a good idea," I said.

"Please," he said.

Knowing it was a mistake but desperate to be near him, I nodded, grabbed my jacket, and shoved my bare feet into my boots. "Mom, I'll be back in a bit."

My mom popped out of the kitchen. "Aren't you going to introduce me to your friend?"

"Jesse, this is my mom. Mom, this is Jesse." I grabbed my purse and opened the front door. "I'll be back later."

I hurried Jesse out of the house, my breath catching in my throat at just the sight of Cash's car in the driveway. Cash would be at work, but it didn't stop me from searching for him in the car anyway.

I climbed into the passenger side as Jesse slid behind the wheel. He pulled out of the driveway, and we drove silently for nearly five minutes before I cleared my throat. "Where are we going?"

"Home," he said.

"No!" Panic made my voice too loud.

"Yes," he said. "You belong with us, Del."

"Jesse, pull the car over!"

He shook his head, and I scowled at him. "Pull the car over right now or I swear I'll call 9-1-1 and tell them you're kidnapping me."

He grinned a little. "Fuck, I've missed you, baby."

"Don't you 'baby' me," I said. "Pull the car over."

"If I do, will you promise to listen to what I have to say?"

I hesitated, and he reached over and squeezed my leg with his warm hand. "Please, Del."

"Fine," I said. "You've got five minutes."

He turned down a side street and parked before unbuckling his seat belt and turning in the seat to face me. His eyes roamed over my face. "I've missed you, Del."

"I've missed you too," I said. "I'm sorry I left without saying goodbye."

He didn't reply, and I took his hand and squeezed it. "I really am sorry, Jesse."

"You shouldn't have left," he said. "I spent the first three days so angry I could barely function."

"I'm sorry," I said. "I had to leave."

"No, you didn't."

"I did," I said. "I don't know what Cash told you, but -"

"Other than telling me you left and moved back in with your parents, he hasn't told me shit," Jesse said. "He's barely spoken a fucking word since you left. He misses you."

I looked away. "I'm sure he doesn't."

"Why do you think that?"

"It doesn't matter, Jesse," I said.

He frowned. "Cash has been a goddamn mess since you left. He hasn't gone to work in four days."

I gaped at him. Cash *always* went to work. The guy loved his job. "You're kidding me."

"I'm not," he said. "Why did you leave, Del?"

I pressed my lips together and blinked back tears. "When Cash and I first got together, he told me not to fall in love with him, that he didn't do conventional relationships, and he wasn't looking for love. I said that was fine. I thought I wouldn't fall in love with him, but I was wrong."

Jesse's tense body relaxed, and he blew his breath out in a harsh rush. "Is that all? Thank fucking Christ."

"Is that all? Jesse, are you listening to me? I'm in love with him, and he's not in love with me. He specifically told me not to -"

"Cash loves you, Del," Jesse said.

My mouth dropped open. "No, he doesn't."

"He does. Listen, I've known Cash for a long time, and he's not a real demonstrative guy when it comes to his feelings, you know? I'm not sure how familiar you are with his family life, but he struggles to express affection or love in a traditional way. After what his family put him through, I understand it, and once you know what they did, you will too."

"I already know," I said.

"Well then, you know why he is the way he is. Just because he doesn't say the words doesn't mean he isn't in love with you. Actions speak louder than words, right?"

I blinked at him. "Cash isn't in love with me, Jesse. He's in love with -"

"He is," Jesse insisted before I could finish. "You love him, and he loves you, so the problem is solved. Move back in before Cash loses his fucking mind, Del."

I stared blankly at him. If anyone was losing their mind, it was Jesse. "Jesse, there's still the issue of you and -"

"I'll move out," he said. "I'll move out and give you and Cash your space. I love Cash, and it's killing me to see him suffering like this."

My jaw dropped again. "Cash loves *you*."

"He does," Jesse agreed. "But he loves you too, and I want him to be happy. You and Cash deserve a chance at happiness, Del. So, are you ready to go back home?"

"Jesse…"

He stared at me, his face a careful mask of neutrality. "This is your chance to have what you want. Take it."

"Jesus Christ, Jesse," I said, "it's not just about me falling in love with Cash."

"What do you mean?"

"I love you too."

His face lit up, and he leaned forward and cupped my face in a hard grip before mashing his mouth against mine. His tongue pushed past my lips, and I returned his kiss eagerly. God, I had missed him.

He pulled his mouth away, and I touched my stinging lips with trembling fingers as he stared at me. "You love me."

"I do," I said. "I love you, Jesse."

"I love you too," he whispered before pressing kisses all over my face.

I started to cry, and he wiped my tears away. "Don't cry, sweet Del. Everything's good."

"It isn't," I sobbed. "Even if all three of us love each other, it will never work."

"Why not?" Jesse asked.

"Because I'm a jealous person," I said. "I feel like a third wheel when I'm with you and Cash. Even if you and Cash aren't jealous, I am. That isn't fair to either of you, and eventually it'll drive a wedge between all of us. I'm not destroying what you and Cash have, Jesse."

He kissed my forehead. "Del, are you jealous because you don't like Cash and me paying attention to each other or jealous because you thought Cash and I loved each other and not you?"

I hesitated, staring wide-eyed at him, as Jesse kissed me again. "Which is it?"

"I – because I didn't think you loved me," I said.

"Well, now you know that we do," he said.

"It isn't that simple."

"It is," he said with maddening certainty.

"It isn't," I insisted. "Jesse, neither of us can even tell our family about our relationship. We're both pretending to be someone we're not. Do you want to live this lie for the rest of your life?"

"I'll tell my family if you do," Jesse said.

My mouth dropped open for a record-breaking third time in less than five minutes. "You've gone crazy!"

He laughed. "Maybe. Listen, we'll figure out the family thing, okay? All that matters is that the three of us have each other. If our families disown us, so fucking what?"

He was acting weirdly cheerful, and I scowled at him. "Why are you being so upbeat about all of this? Why do you suddenly not care what your family thinks?"

"Del," Jesse said, "do you have any idea the hell I've gone

through the last week? The woman I love left without saying goodbye, and the man I love is losing his mind. I drove here fully expecting to walk away from both of you and spend the rest of my life apart from the two people I love. A future where my parents know I'm bi is a fucking cakewalk compared to the future I was imagining."

"Oh, Jesse," I said before throwing my arms around him. I hugged him hard. "I'm so sorry."

"I know," he said. "Let me take you home, Del. Neither Cash nor I can live without you. We'll make it work. I promise."

"Okay," I said.

"Really?"

"Yes."

He hugged me again before settling in his seat and buckling his seat belt. He started the car and pulled out into the street.

"I should go to my parents and grab my things," I said.

"Later. I want to get you home to Cash," he said. "By the way, I told the guys I wanted to bring you into the band, and they agreed."

"I can't sing with you guys, Jesse."

"Why not? You don't have a job anymore, remember?"

"I can get another waitress job," I said.

He shrugged. "Probably, but at least think about the offer, okay? You have a great voice, and we sound amazing together. We've been wanting to change our sound for a while now."

"I'll think about it," I promised as I stared out the windshield. My stomach was churning with a combination of hope and anxiety. As if he sensed it, Jesse reached out and grabbed my hand before squeezing it reassuringly.

"Cash is going to be happy to see you. I promise."

"I hope so," I said.

"Are you ready?" Jesse asked as the elevator doors opened.

I nodded and took off my jacket and boots before taking Jesse's hand. "Where's Cash?"

"Probably in his bedroom. He hasn't left it for the last two days," he said. He led me toward the bedroom, giving me a gentle tug when I slowed down. "It'll be good, Del. You'll see."

"I hope you're right about Cash being in love with me. If not, this is about to get really fucking awkward," I said.

He just smiled and knocked on the bedroom door before opening it. "Cash? I have a surprise for you."

He pulled me into the bedroom, and I stared at Cash. He stood at the glass wall, wearing just a pair of jeans, and stared out the window. There was a glass in his hand, and he drained the liquid in it before pouring himself another drink from the bottle of Scotch that was on the narrow table next to the window.

"Go away, Jesse," he said. "I'm not interested."

Jesse squeezed my hand and made a 'go on' motion. I took a deep breath and said timidly, "Hello, Cash."

Cash stiffened, his hand tightening on the glass in his hand before he pivoted and stared at me. I winced a little. He looked terrible. The usual scruff on his jaw was a dark beard, and his eyes were bloodshot with dark circles beneath them.

"Little lamb?" He set the glass on the table.

"Hi," I said. Warmth was flooding through me at the sound of my nickname, and I took a hesitant step forward. "Cash, I'm sorry I -"

Cash made a strangled noise deep in his throat and charged forward. I squeaked in surprise when he picked me up and hugged me so hard I thought I heard my ribs cracking in protest.

"Cash," I gasped, "can't breathe!"

"I'm sorry," he said before pressing kisses against my face. "I'm so sorry."

"I'm sorry," I said. "I shouldn't have left."

"I shouldn't have let you leave," he said before kissing me hard on the mouth.

I moaned with pleasure and reached down to cup his cock through his jeans. I rubbed him until he was hard and pressing against the denim.

"Del, we need to talk," he moaned.

"Sex now, talk later," I said before groping behind me. "Jesse, come here."

Jesse pressed up against me and kissed the top of my head before smiling at Cash. Cash reached over me and cupped Jesse's head, kissing him hard on the mouth. "Thank you, Jesse."

"You're welcome. Now, let's get her naked."

I laughed as Jesse yanked my t-shirt over my head. He unclasped my bra as Cash unbuttoned my jeans and pushed them and my panties down my legs. Jesse braced me as Cash pulled them off my feet and tossed them aside. I stood naked between them, flushing with pleasure at the looks of need and desire on both their faces.

"Jesse," Cash said hoarsely, "strip and get on your knees."

"Yes, sir," Jesse said. He stripped off his clothes as Cash shoved his jeans down his legs. He was naked under them, and I wrapped my hand around his thick cock, rubbing firmly as he moaned.

"I've missed your big cock," I said.

"I've missed you," he whispered before kissing me.

"Me too," I said breathlessly when he released my mouth.

Jesse was on his knees behind me, and Cash turned me to face him. He cupped my breasts and teased my nipples as he smiled at Jesse. "Eat her pussy, Jesse."

"Yes, sir," Jesse said.

I spread my legs and made a loud squeal of delight at the first touch of Jesse's warm tongue. Cash's big hand circled my throat, and he pulled me against him as he sucked on my earlobe. His cock was pressing against my ass, and I rubbed against it eagerly.

"Hold still, baby," Jesse growled before giving my thigh a light slap.

I jerked, and Cash reached between us to squeeze my ass. "You were a very bad girl for leaving us, little lamb. Weren't you?"

"Yes," I moaned as Jesse rubbed his tongue stud against my clit.

"What do bad girls get?"

"A spanking?" I said hopefully.

Cash's laughter washed over me, warming my body as much as Jesse's mouth on my pussy did. "That's right, little lamb.

I moaned again and wiggled against Jesse's tongue. I was about three seconds from coming, and I muttered a curse when Cash said, "Jesse, stop."

He stopped immediately, and I pouted down at him. "Jesse, please."

"No, baby. Not yet," he said.

He stood, and I stared at his cock, my mouth nearly starting to water.

"Bend over, Del," Cash said. He pressed on my back with one hand, keeping his other hand clamped firmly on my hip.

I bent over obediently. My mouth was level with Jesse's cock, and it took all of my willpower not to suck on him.

Jesse's hands were in my hair, stroking and tugging lightly, and he said hoarsely, "Cash, please."

"Suck Jesse's cock, little lamb," Cash demanded.

I obeyed immediately, sucking on Jesse's cock like a

woman possessed. Jesse's hips bucked forward, and he made a loud groan as he held my hair in a loose ponytail. "Fuck, I've missed your hot little mouth, baby."

Cash was pushing my legs apart, and at the first feel of his cock nudging the opening of my pussy, I moaned around Jesse's cock and ground myself against Cash. He squeezed my hip and thrust hard into me, knocking me forward until my nose was pressed against Jesse's pubic hair.

Jesse cried out, his fist tightening in my hair before he took a step back. I took a gasping breath of air and sucked at his cock again as Cash thrust back and forth.

Both men were thrusting roughly, and I clung to Jesse's hips as Cash slapped my ass hard. I made a muffled squeal and clenched my pussy around Cash's cock. He groaned and spanked me again and again. The bite of pain enhanced my pleasure, and I screamed around Jesse's cock as Cash slapped me a final time and my orgasm roared through me.

"Fuck!" Jesse shouted as his hips bucked forward. He came in my mouth, and I swallowed the hot spurts of liquid eagerly. Cash pumped in and out for another thirty seconds before throwing his head back and making a harsh, short howl of pleasure. He held my hips as my pussy squeezed his cock rhythmically.

They pulled out of my pussy and mouth at the same time, and I would have fallen flat on my face if Cash hadn't lifted me into his arms. He nuzzled my throat as he carried me to the bed and placed me on my stomach. Jesse slid into the bed on my left as Cash pulled a bottle from the nightstand.

I closed my eyes and enjoyed the attention as both men rubbed the cool liquid into my stinging ass before running their hands up and down my back. The bed dipped as they lay down on either side of me. I was warm and relaxed and sleepy, but I obeyed Cash when he said, "Turn over, little lamb."

I smiled happily and kissed each of them before they nestled their heads in the curve of my neck. I rubbed their shoulders as they cupped my breasts and stroked my skin with their rough hands.

"That was amazing," I said dreamily. "Thank you."

"Del," Cash said. I opened my eyes. He leaned over me, tracing my collarbone with the tip of one finger. He hesitated, and I stroked his dark beard.

"I like your beard," I said.

He smiled a little. "Thanks."

Jesse snorted. "I'm not so fond of the beard."

I grinned at him. "I was just trying to be polite. We can pin him down and shave it off later."

Jesse laughed, but Cash continued to stare solemnly at me. My stomach twisted, and I swallowed nervously. "Cash, what's wrong?"

"I should have told you that I," he hesitated again and glanced at Jesse, who gave him an encouraging look, "I should have told you that I loved you too. I'm sorry."

I started to cry, and he kissed me. "Don't cry, little lamb."

"I love you," I whispered. "I love you and I love Jesse and I'm so sorry I left."

Cash nuzzled my throat, and we both laughed when Jesse said, "I told you he loved you."

"Quiet, you." I poked him in his hard abdomen. He caught my hand and lifted it to his mouth to press a kiss against my palm.

"Listen, Del, don't expect Cash to be making daily declarations of love. I've been with him for years, and he's said it maybe three times to me," Jesse said.

"I don't need daily declarations," I said before smiling at Cash. "I don't, okay?"

Cash nodded, and I didn't think I was imagining the look

of relief that flickered across his face. "You're moving back in with us."

It was more of a statement than a question, but I nodded anyway. "Yes, as long as you don't mind that I'm currently unemployed."

"You're not." Jesse grinned at Cash. "She's joining the band."

"I didn't say that," I protested as Cash smiled at me.

"I think that's a great idea, little lamb."

I just shrugged and took Cash and Jesse's hands in each of mine. "This isn't going to be easy, is it?"

"Probably not," Cash said, "but we'll make it work."

"That's what I said," Jesse said. "Besides, it won't be as difficult as you think. We love each other, that's what matters."

"Yes," I agreed as Cash smiled at both of us. "That's exactly what matters."

Keep reading for an excerpt from Ramona Gray's novella, "The Mechanic".

THE MECHANIC EXCERPT

Copyright © 2018 Ramona Gray

Jack

"Are you fucking kidding me?"

I stared at the woman in front of me. Never once in my fucking life did I believe that Lily "Ice Queen" Carson would be standing in the tiny shithole of a room I called an office. The cement walls used to be white, but years of dirt and grease had turned them the colour of a roach. The smell was a hellish combination of oil, gas, and the leftover spaghetti I had heated up for lunch.

I leaned against my desk and folded my arms across my chest. Her gaze followed the motion, and I watched a muscle tick in her temple and a flush rise in her cheeks. I'm in good shape. Years of being a grease monkey and spending weekends at the local boxing gym have made my body hard. I reached down and adjusted my dick, grinning when the flush turned to a bright red stain.

The woman standing in front of me might have been a

rich, stuck-up ice queen that I didn't have a chance in hell with, but fuck did she get my motor running. She had since fucking high school.

Of course, she wasn't exactly rich anymore, was she?

I folded my arms back over my chest. "I don't do payment plans."

That red stain faded from her cheeks, leaving her looking pale and sick. I scratched at the two days' worth of stubble on my jaw.

"But, uh, Tom Wilk said that you did payment plans. He told me you didn't have a problem with it." She fidgeted with the strap of her purse.

I lowered my gaze to her tits. They were big and firm, and I wondered not for the first time what her nipples looked like. What would it look like to have my dick sliding between those lush titties? I hadn't been this close to her since I sat behind her in biology class in high school. Why would I be? She was the daughter of the richest man in town, and I was the son of the drunkest.

Or rather, we had been. My cunt of an old man had been dead for two years, and her old man had lost everything thanks to insider trading. He was currently enjoying life in some white-collar minimum security prison, and little Miss Rich Bitch was suddenly not so rich.

Her mother had left town about six months after her father went to prison. The rumour was that she'd met some new rich asshole willing to give her whatever she wanted just for a daily go at her pussy. In the two years since then, I'd often wondered why Lily didn't go with her. There was nothing in this town for her, and without her daddy's money, her popularity had disappeared faster than a dick in a whore's mouth. Her boyfriend had dumped her, her mansion on the west side of town had gone to foreclosure, and all her fancy friends had abandoned her. Now, she lived in an old trailer in the worst part of town and waitressed at a local dive bar.

Her arms folded across her tits, and I lifted my gaze to her face. She was even paler, and her big blue eyes were watering with unshed tears. I felt a twinge of guilt that I immediately tamped down. Her money problems weren't my problem. I had a business to run.

"He was fucking with you."

"I – what?" she said.

"Tom was fucking with you. I don't do payment plans." I grabbed the invoice from my desk and tapped the number on the bottom. "Your piece-of-shit car needed a lot of work to get it running. Seven hundred dollars' worth, in fact."

"Mr. Williams, I don't have seven hundred dollars. I believed that you did payment plans. Could you – I mean, would you consider doing a payment plan just this once? I could pay you fifty dollars a month with interest, of course."

"No. Pay me today, or your car stays in my shop until you bring me the seven hundred."

She chewed at her bottom lip. "Please. I need my car to get to work every day. If I'm fired, I won't have the money to pay you. But if you let me take my car and do a payment plan, you'll get your money. I swear. Please, Mr. Williams. I need this job. You know how hard it is to find work in this town."

"I think you have me confused with someone who gives a fuck about your problems."

The hell of it was, I was tempted to give her a payment plan. Fuck, I was tempted just to let her take the damn car for free. I was a bastard, always had been and always would be, but something about Lily Carson made me want to be soft with her. Made me want to hold her in my arms and tell her everything would be fine. I would take care of her. I'd make sure she -

I snorted inwardly. Fuck me. I was like a goddamn Hall-mark movie now. All because of a former rich girl's tears.

Those tears were sliding down her cheeks now, her soft-looking lips trembling. She was thinner now than in high school, but in less of an I'm-trying-to-look-like-a-stick-thin-model way and more of an I-don't-have-enough-to-eat way.

She wiped the tears away before taking a deep breath. A look of weary resignation mixed with a 'here we go again' expression crossed her face.

"Mr. Williams, I realize that I treated you horribly in high school and would like to apologize for it. It is not an excuse, but I was young and immature and a self-absorbed bitch. I am deeply sorry for what I said and did to you when we attended Winston High together. My behaviour and actions are inexcusable, but I truly am remorseful about my behaviour."

Her little speech had an air of robotic rehearsal to it. I cocked my head and said, "How many times have you done this little song and dance with the assholes in this town when you needed something?"

Her lips compressed into a thin line. "Many."

"It ever work?"

"Yes. Because I'm being sincere."

"Bullshit. You're saying what you think we want to hear and nothing more."

"That isn't true," she said. "I am very sorry for my past behaviour toward you. I'm hoping you can find it in your heart to forgive me and maybe just this once, let me do a payment plan with your business."

She might be broke flatter than piss on a platter now, but she still talked like she was Miss Fucking Fancy Pants. I actually admired her for it. Her expensive clothes and jewels were long gone. Her silver BMW was replaced by a Honda Accord that was being held together with spit, duct tape and a goddamn prayer, and she worked at a bar that she would never have stepped foot in, in her previous life, but she still talked like the rich little princess she used to be.

And fuck did it make my dick harder than a mother-fucking rock.

Before I could lose my fucking mind and just give her the goddamn car, I shut down the weird part of me that wanted to help her. Threw it deep and locked away the key. The woman in front of me didn't give a shit about me. Besides, my interest in her was purely physical. Nothing else.

"Well," I drawled as I leaned back against my desk, "I appreciate the apology, but it won't pay my bills. Seven hundred, Ice Queen, or your car stays here."

A look of pure panic flickered across her face. It made my pulse speed up and my body tense in unexpected solidarity. I distracted myself by staring at her tits again. Fuck, I'd give my left nut to watch those big tits bouncing as I fucked her hard and rough. She'd look so fucking hot cumming all over my dick.

Of course, she had the nickname of Ice Queen for a reason. She flirted plenty with the guys in high school she'd deemed worthy, but she never let any of them into her silk panties. At least not according to the rampant gossip that ran through the high school. Her senior year, she started dating Isaac Morris and they continued to date after high school.

He had dumped her the minute her father was found guilty. I don't know what she did to piss him off, but he hadn't been shy about sharing the details of their sex life once they were over. According to that dickwad, she was frigid as a goddamn freezer. I'd overheard him telling a bunch of his asshole friends at Ren's bar about her shortcomings in the sack and how she refused to fuck him more than once a week. Two months after they broke up, everyone in town knew all about her aversion to sex and the nickname Ice Queen was born.

I forced my gaze away from her tits and back to her face. She was still standing near the door to my office, but the panic had been replaced with cold and calculating desperation. She reached out and shut the door. She didn't need to bother. It was the end of the day, and I was the only one left in the shop, but I didn't say anything as she dropped her cheap purse on my office floor.

She walked slowly toward me with that cold desperation still stamped all over her pretty face, and my dick jerked in my jeans when she placed one soft hand on my chest. Fuck, did she smell good. Like strawberries. I suppressed my groan when she traced her hand back and forth over my chest. Even through my t-shirt, I could feel the heat of her hand.

I stared at her mouth and wondered how those lips would look stretched around my fat dick. I couldn't control my filthy thoughts around the Ice Queen, no matter how hard I tried.

Not that I was trying all that fucking hard.

"Mr. Williams, perhaps we can come up with a different idea of how I can pay you for my car repairs."

The heat from her hand, her sweet scent and the closeness of her tits to my chest had me as horny as a teenager. I could barely fucking think straight. I stared at her, wondering what the hell she was talking about.

With that hard light of desperation in her eyes, she said, "What do you think?"

"What do I think about what?" I said stupidly.

She chewed on her bottom lip before deliberately dropping her gaze to my cock. It was hard and tenting the front of my jeans, and I could see the red rising from her chest up her neck.

"I'll give you my mouth," she said.

What the fuck was I missing? I wasn't a stupid man, but apparently, being this close to Lily made my brain mush.

"You'll give me your mouth," I repeated.

"Yes, I'll... I'll suck your penis in exchange for the work you did on my car."

My mouth dropped open so fucking wide you could have shoved a dick into it.

ABOUT THE AUTHOR

Ramona Gray is a Canadian romance author. She currently lives in Alberta with her awesome husband and her super cute dog. She's addicted to home improvement shows, good coffee, and reading and writing about the steamier moments in life.

For more information about Ramona, check out her website at

www.ramonagray.ca

- facebook.com/RamonaGrayBooks
- instagram.com/ramonagrayauthor
- amazon.com/Ramona-Gray/e/B00OD26SAM
- bookbub.com/profile/ramona-gray

ALSO BY RAMONA GRAY

Individual Books

The Escort

Saving Jax

Sharing Del

Filthy Appeal

Forbidden Bliss

The Assistant Series

The Assistant

One Night

The Boss

Shadow Security Series

Dead of Night

Edge of Night

Dark of Night

End of Night

Undeniable Series

Undeniably His

Undeniably Hers

Undeniably Theirs

Working Men Series

The Mechanic

The Carpenter

The Bartender